HAMISH
AND THE
MONSTER PATROL

Look Out For

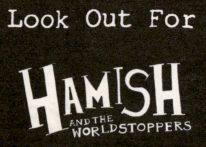

HAMISH AND THE **WORLDSTOPPERS**

HAMISH AND THE **NEVERPEOPLE**

HAMISH AND THE **GRAVITYBURP**

HAMISH AND THE **BABY BOOM!**

HAMISH And the **TERRIBLE TERRIBLE CHRISTMAS** And other Stories

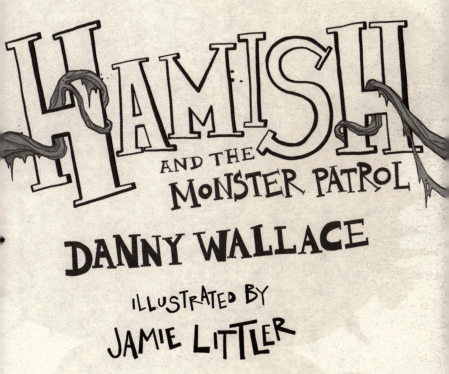

HAMISH
AND THE
MONSTER PATROL

DANNY WALLACE

ILLUSTRATED BY
JAMIE LITTLER

SIMON & SCHUSTER
LONDON NEW YORK SYDNEY TORONTO NEW DELHI STARKLEY

First published in Great Britain in 2019 by Simon and Schuster UK Ltd
A CBS COMPANY

Text Copyright © 2019 Danny Wallace
Illustrations Copyright © 2019 Jamie Littler

1 3 5 7 9 10 8 6 4 2

Simon & Schuster UK Ltd
1st Floor, 222 Gray's Inn Road
London
WC1X 8HB

www.simonandschuster.co.uk

Simon & Schuster Australia, Sydney
Simon & Schuster India, New Delhi

A CIP catalogue record for this book is
available from the British Library.
PB ISBN 978-1-4711-6786-7
eBook ISBN 978-1-4711-6785-0

Printed and bound by CPI Group (UK)
Ltd, Croydon, CR0 4YY
Simon & Schuster UK Ltd are committed to
sourcing paper that is made from wood grown
in sustainable forests and supports the Forest
Stewardship Council, the leading international forest
certification organisation. Our books displaying the
FSC logo are printed on FSC certified paper.

MIX
Paper from
responsible sources
FSC® C020471

For Lola and Darcy –
DW

ORIENT EXPRESS

EBW09 – Venice

LAST NIGHT'S News

Thursday, 30 1982

Fiji

MISSING TRAVEL WRITER STILL MISSING
(AS OF LAST NIGHT)

The noted travel writer known simply as 'Lydia' is still nowhere to be found (as of last night)! Her last review, for Hotel Empanada, a resort in the middle of the Amazon rainforest, was a curiously-written piece which didn't seem to make much sense.

Perhaps she simply went mad, said experts, last night.

Lydia has travelled everywhere from the tallest mountains of the Andes to Kettering, and is one of the country's best-travelled writers. Her raft of talents include paragliding,

hand-to-hand combat, sharpshooting, speedboat driving and lots of other things that don't seem particularly necessary for being a travel writer.

Her disappearance is highly unusual. Or at least it still was, last night.

00594

ADMISSION
ADMIT ONE THIS DATE ONLY

taj mahal
ADMIT ONE

ALCATE
CALIFORNIA

ADMIT NO

TOKYO
IMMIGRATION

WERE-CAT

RE A WEREWOLF BUT A CAT. HUGE
TEETH. SHARP CLAWS. CANNOT BE
TAMED WITH WARM STRAWBERRY MILK.
(DO NOT ATTEMPT TO DO SO AGAIN)

BANSHEE BAT

SIZE OF AN AUSTIN AMBASSADOR. VERY BAD
ATTITUDE WHEN WOKEN. TIP: DO NOT CLIMB
ON TOP OF ONE. YOU WILL END UP 200
MILES AWAY AND EXTREMELY JET-LAGGED.

THE STORMWORM

GIANT WORM THING. SPEAKS ORCADIAN. ITS TEETH ARE SUPPOSED TO HAVE
FALLEN OUT AND TURNED INTO ISLANDS. THIS IS ABSOLUTE NONSENSE!

GRÜNEWAL

EYKJAVIK

HOTEL
EMPANADA

ROOM SERVICE MENU

Coconut

Coconut water

Coconut nut

Cocoa

Nuts

Coconut nut bar

Please advise the kitchen of
any coconut allergies.

AZ

MING

NEPAL NEPAL NEPAL NEPAL

THIS MIGHT BE BIGFOOT
OR IT MIGHT JUST BE A
BIG FOOT. ALSO, WHAT IS
THE PLURAL OF BIGFOOT, IS IT
BIGFOOTS OR IS IT BIGFEET?
MUST CHECK.

HOTEL

1

Days Until Arrival: 7

Everybody worries about monsters coming, don't they?

Horrible monsters rushing through the door. Nasty monsters bursting through the window. Monsters running down the street.

But can I tell you what is even more worrying than that?

What's more frightening?

More terrifying?

More awful?

In fact, worse in every single way?

When that monster is still *miles* away.

What do you mean, that doesn't sound as bad?

Think about it.

You know it's coming.

You know it's on its way, but you don't know how to stop it.

One heavy foot after the other, it moves towards you.

CLUNK.

THUNK.

BLUNK.

Never distracted. Never slowing. Always coming.

That's a terrifying thought, isn't it? Knowing a monster is on its way, even as you sleep, but that you can't do anything about it?

Well, that, my young and stinky friend, has been the everyday reality for the people of the small town of Starkley for some time now. Since right after Christmas, in fact, and on through all the dark January nights, with no hope on the horizon to brighten them.

No one knows what the monster is.

No one knows what it wants.

But everyone knows it is coming.

Steadily.

Purposefully.

Definitely.

Ever since the day it was first spotted on a radar system,

moving very slowly indeed through the ocean, scientists have been tracking this ever-growing red dot. Somewhere deep under the swirling water, this enormous unspeakable thing is moving, with clear intention, in the direction of Starkley.

What is it? What does it want? How long until it's here?

Can you imagine living every day under the weight of questions like that?

The real danger, of course, is that you get used to the fear. You start to ignore the creeping threat, until one day the monster arrives and it's then you realise you have no fight left.

So what would you do?

Run?

Some people already have.

Hide?

But what if it finds you?

Stay where you are and eat a sandwich and hope for the best?

A nice idea, but not exactly what I'd call a plan . . .

All this impending doom has changed the once-cheerful, once-boring town of Starkley beyond recognition.

In fact, I have to wonder if you'd recognise it at all.

2

DAYS UNTIL ARRIVAL: 6

It was just after teatime, which meant that Hamish Ellerby really had to hurry if he was going to get home before the Gate shut.

Hamish had been at his karate class at the leisure centre in Frinkley as usual – Mum said it was important to do normal things, even if things weren't normal at all any more – but after class he'd had a go on the arcades and lost track of time. Now he was cycling quicker than he ever had before, battling against a chill wind that seemed to threaten snow. **'Slow down, Hamish!'** shouted his best friend, Alice, pedalling behind him. 'We've got plenty of time!'

But Hamish knew that the Siren would be going off soon, and if they didn't get through the Gate before that happened, they'd be locked out of Starkley all night.

It began to rain. Fat, freezing drops of rain. The river was swollen and noisy as they rode over the old grey bridge towards Checkpoint Gamma.

This was all new – these checkpoints and barriers – and they hadn't been Starkley's idea. But each night, all the people in the town who had chosen to stay in Starkley, despite The News, had to make sure they were all signed in.

People called the ever-nearing threat 'The News' because it seemed better than calling it 'The Monster' or 'The Upcoming Season of Destruction' or anything else like that.

Hamish couldn't quite believe there was less than a week to go . . .

When the monster had been spotted on the radar, the rest of the country had decided that the safest thing to do would be to shut Starkley off. Oh, they could come and go during the day, but they'd lock the doors at night, when monsters usually come out. And they'd limit deliveries, because maybe if life wasn't so cushy in Starkley, more people would leave and the problem might just go away. You have to be cruel to be kind, they said.

And let's be honest: this was hardly the first time Starkley had made a spectacle of itself, was it? Trouble seemed to always be just around the corner for the small town. It had only been a few months since the last battle with those awful beasts the Terribles, who had somehow brainwashed all the town's infants to rise up and riot. And before that, Starkley had fallen foul of the invasion of the Venus spytraps, and before that the giant, time-pausing WorldStoppers. And let's not forget those brain-zapping Hypnobots!

So, deep down, the rest of the country wasn't particularly happy that Starkley had somehow managed to attract yet another monster. Some people had even started protesting outside Parliament, and there's nothing politicians hate more than that. People mad e banners and put up posters saying things like . . .

Oi, Starkley!
It's all very well saving the world all the time, but maybe if you weren't QUITE so attractive to monsters then you wouldn't NEED to!

STOP BRINGING IN MONSTERS! I DON'T LIKE THEM!

CUT STARKLEY OFF!

R.I.P. STARKELEY

Others said that maybe Starkley should be taught a lesson about always wanting to be the centre of attention. 'Evening, Hamish. Evening, Alice,' said a border guard, about to bring down a barrier. 'Just in time...'

Hamish cruised into the town square, relieved to have made it, and skidded to a halt by the town clock. Alice stopped next to him. The rain was falling more heavily now and both kids watched as it bounced off the tin metal roof of the Control Tower by the clock and spattered on to the sandbags below. There were sandbags everywhere now; experts had started to worry that Starkley could flood if the monster rose out of the sea fast enough. It was right on the coast, after all. 'Oh, well,' Madame Cous Cous had said when she heard. 'Keep Calm and Carry a Snorkel!'

The Central Speaker **HOOOOONKED** three times, to tell everyone that it was getting close to curfew time. A lot of the grown-ups would be sitting around right now, arguing about what to do. All the kids had to be indoors soon. The next time the Central Speaker honked, the Child Curfew would start. Parents wanted their kids right where they could see them, mainly because no one fancied going out in the dark any more. Without knowing quite what this monster was, it was easy for rumours to swirl, and for people to drive themselves crazy with questions. What if it sped up? What if there were others coming from different directions? Wait – did I turn off the kitchen tap?

Belasko had increased its presence in Starkley, led, of course, by their very best agent, Hamish's dad, Angus Ellerby. The super-spy agency had always come to help Starkley before and this emergency was no different – there were agents all over the place, coming up with plans and researching. They weren't just going to sit about, waiting for the monster to arrive. The most important thing was to find out just what the monster was, but, so far, none of their plans to get a closer look had worked.

They'd sent jets flying across the water, but they'd been

repelled by bad weather.

They'd sailed boats out, but their agents never returned.

They'd tried a submarine, but whatever was heading their way seemed surrounded by a thick black underwater cloud that enveloped it.

And they couldn't just shoot missiles at the monster randomly, because what if they hit some fish, or a whale?

Nothing seemed to be working, so until they could identify the monster heading towards them, all they could do was prepare Starkley for the worst.

Seeing all these **Belasko** agents everywhere was supposed to make everyone feel better. But it just made people realise how much things had changed.

Hamish looked up at the giant electronic billboard that now dominated the town square.

It said:

Hamish's tummy sank. The best guess **Belasko** had was that in just six days – if it kept going at the speed it was going – the monster would be here.

And in the morning it would say **5**.

'See you at school tomorrow,' said Alice. 'I'd better get home. Mum's making weak lentil soup. Bleurgh.'

'See you tomorrow,' Hamish said. 'We can still crack this.'

Alice nodded, trying to remain positive. But she knew the sad truth. That unless they came up with something soon, the unthinkable would happen. Even the bravest souls would have to abandon Starkley.

Hamish had reason to be hopeful, though.

'I just mean,' he said, 'what with your family history and everything . . .'

Over Christmas, Alice had done some digging into her family tree and she'd found out something extraordinary about her grandmother. Alice had always thought that Granny Lydia had disappeared on a travel-writing trip, but actually Lydia been a monster hunter! It had been a super-cool secret to discover and Alice had been proud to share her findings with her friends in the **PDF**. But, ever since the dot on the radar had been spotted, her best friends seemed to think that Alice should have all the answers. After all, monster hunting ran in her blood. And she had a stripe in her hair, just like her grandma. They were peas in a pod! It was a lot of pressure for poor Alice.

'Yeah . . . maybe we can come up with something,' she said with a half-smile at her friend. It was weird, something seemed to have changed between them recently. Hamish seemed much quieter these days. Alice worried that Hamish was disappointed in her because this 'thing' was coming and even with her monster-hunting genes Alice couldn't come up with a plan.

Hamish watched her cycle away in the rain.

The Central Speaker honked again.

He turned his bike around and sped home, where he ate his tea, went to bed early, and had the dream again.

Because what Alice didn't know was that Hamish had secret worries of his own . . .

THE DREAM

Even before the monster had started making its way to Starkley, Hamish had been having the same dream night after night. And tonight was no different. The dream began as it always did . . .

He's floating high over the ocean . . . far from town, as his best friends in the world stand on the cliffs and stare up at him.

Alice, the girl with the stripe in her hair who'd started their gang in the first place.

Elliot and Clover, the genius and the master of disguise.

Buster, the technical whizz whose inventions always came in handy in the battle against evil.

Venk, whose skills were less easy to define, but who could make a cracking sandwich.

Hamish drifts backwards, his pals growing smaller and smaller . . .

Suddenly, the looks on their faces change, and they start to wave at Hamish, begging him to stop floating, begging him to come back to them, jumping up and down and shouting . . .

But Hamish can't respond . . . the cold air tightens his throat as he turns to face the distance.

He has no choice.

The wind rises and the air gets colder still as he begins to fly. Fast.

The sky darkens and the wind gets harder, like nature itself is warning him to go no further. As if it's trying to scare him into turning back.

But still he carries on, unable to do anything about it at all. Like he is being pulled through the air, dragged through the clouds.

Almost as if there is an invisible fist around him.

He starts to fight, realising this is a mistake, kicking against nothing.

Black clouds around him swirl. Lightning strikes.

And then—

3

DAYS UNTIL ARRIVAL: 5

Hamish woke with a start.

Five days. Oh, no.

There was no need for an alarm clock these days. The honks of the Central Speaker woke the whole town up. Soon he would hear the rumble of trucks as the Gate opened and the daily food supplies arrived. Maybe he'd pop down Lord of the Fries later . . . if there were enough potatoes. Hamish remembered the last battered sausage and curry sauce he'd had there – weeks ago! – and his mouth began to salivate. Nowadays, it was mainly chips and lentils. Still, at least they had chips. Before Dad had to spend quite so much time at **Belasko** he'd said to Hamish, 'Don't worry. Society will only crumble the day you can't get chips!'

Hamish sat up and thought about his dream. He never felt like he got to the end. It was all building up to something, but he could never work out what was really going on. Like when he listened to a rambling speech about steam trains or the history of wallpaper by his teacher, Mr Longblather.

The Central Speaker stopped its morning honks and Hamish wondered how much closer the monster had crept to Starkley overnight. Apparently it moved very slowly. Somehow that made it even scarier. But recently the experts had detected a minor increase in speed, which wasn't a good sign. Hamish's tummy sank.

And do you know why?

Not because he was scared. And not because he was sad. And not because he really wanted a battered sausage.

But because he felt guilty.

Hamish had a secret. You know how secrets can weigh you down? Well, Hamish's was a heavy secret. One he longed to tell his friends but didn't have the courage to. He wished he could be more like Alice, who was so proud when she discovered her grandma's secret. He didn't see that maybe Alice had her own problems to deal with. He just felt that he, Hamish Ellerby, had nothing to be proud of.

Because Hamish had discovered something very confusing, and it was not about his grandma. It was about his nemesis, **Axel Scarmarsh**. The man who seemed to have singled out Starkley for destruction time and time again. The man whose name struck fear into his heart. Perhaps even the man who was sending this monster. Hamish had found what his dad had told him so hard to believe. He'd even denied it could be true. But he had been forced to accept the grim and unwelcome fact: the man he feared most was also his uncle.

'See you later, chicken!' said Mum as Hamish grabbed his bag and strode out of 13 Lovelock Close and headed off to school. Before the lockdown, his street was always busy, even early in the morning. Sure, there would normally be glass everywhere from where the milkwoman, Margarine Crinkle, had dropped all her bottles. And Hamish would usually have to wait for the whole of the Ramsface family to pile into their neon fawn-coloured minivan and leave their driveway before he could safely make his way down the road. But since The News, lots of people had decided to leave Starkley and that meant that it felt very quiet indeed. The ones that left said it was just for a while, but Hamish wasn't so sure. The people who'd stayed were the people who really loved Starkley. The ones who were making a stand. The ones who couldn't leave at a time when they were needed most. But the ones that Hamish knew would eventually have to.

Hamish's family would stay for as long as they could. Same with Alice's. Buster's, Venk's, Elliot's, and Clover's too. Even Grenville Bile's family refused to leave, although that was mainly because his mum, the Postmaster, had very little work to do these days and knew when she was on to a winner.

Hamish rounded the corner and passed Lord of the Fries. There was a new sign outside that read:

He reached Winterbourne School. With so many families leaving Starkley, school attendance was at an all-time low. Many of the windows had been boarded up because they only needed to use a few classrooms. There was barbed wire around the fence. There was no noise from the playground. There were no ball games, no screams, no laughter. The kids that were still coming to school just stood around talking quietly about things they'd heard their parents saying and the various rumours flying around about The News. It made a lot of people very nervous. The future can be scary when everything changes and you don't know what's going to happen next.

Hamish took a deep breath. He knew what was going to happen next.

And it wasn't good.

It was geography.

4

DAYS UNTIL ARRIVAL:
STILL 5

'Right!' said Mr Longblather, adjusting his polyester tie and standing by his whiteboard. 'We never did finish that lesson on soil erosion!'

There were groans all round. Apparently, your town being threatened by an enormous sea monster didn't mean you could skip school. Hamish looked around the class. So many empty desks. His friend Robin had been the first kid to get yanked out of school by his mum. And that was before they even suspected it was a monster. Robin's mum had just heard about a red dot on a radar thousands of miles away, and boom – she'd bought a two-bedroom bungalow in Thrunkley and retrained as a butcher.

'Please, Mr Longblather,' said Elliot, his hand straining in the air. 'Could we talk about the Gulf of Mexico?'

Mr Longblather rolled his eyes.

'We've been through this a thousand times,' said Mr Longblather. 'Whatever the creature is, it began its life in the Gulf of Mexico.'

'Which formed three hundred million years ago as a result of plate tectonics!' yelled Elliot, delighted with himself, and holding up a large poster he'd made in his spare time to explain what the heck that meant.

'The creature then dragged itself along the seabed,' said Mr Longblather, repeating himself for what seemed like the thousandth time, 'and it grew to a size big enough to be spotted by radar. It changed course once and once only.'

To head straight from the Gulf of Mexico in the direction of Starkley!' yelled Elliot again, delighted, and flipping his poster round to show a map of the monster's route.

'I love Mexican food,' said Grenville, whose favourite thing in the world was a Mexican wrestler known as 'the Prawn'.

'Name three Mexican foods,' said Clover, not believing him for a second.

'Easy,' said Grenville. 'Mexican eggs, Mexican dips and Mexican chips.'

Grenville had obviously been doing quite a lot of research

on the culture. His love of El Gamba was all-encompassing. 'To be like the prawn,' he would tell anyone who would listen, 'you have to *think* like a prawn!'

And then he would explain the PRAWN PUNCH! and the **SHRIMP SHRUG!** and the *GAMBA GAMBLE!* and the totally classic PRAWN TOSS! and tell them about a million prawn facts and then they'd get bored and fall asleep. Grenville had even paid Clover six Chomps and a gargantuan gobstopper to make his El Gamba costume far more elaborate and impressive. And she had done quite the job! He didn't just have a standard mask and cape these days – he had a hot-pink bodysuit and Clover had plans for eyes and antennae too!

'Yes, well, anyway, back to soil erosion,' said Mr Longblather.

Hamish wondered how else they might distract Mr Longblather from talking about soil erosion, because Mr Longblather was one of those teachers you could quite easily divert to another topic. All you had to do was say something like, 'Can you tell us about what trains were like when you were a kid?' and before you knew it, he'd spent forty minutes talking about the history of the railway network and totally forgotten to give you the homework he'd been planning.

But then a hand shot up for a different reason.

'What about the Amazon?' asked Alice. 'Can we talk about the Amazon again?'

Mr Longblather sighed.

'This is not a "greatest hits" class,' he said, flattening his moustache down. 'I don't take requests, Miss Shepherd.'

Hamish smiled at Alice. She had become totally obsessed with the Amazon rainforest ever since she'd discovered the truth about her grandma. She was desperate for more information. Even things she'd heard before. She loved to imagine her mysterious grandma hunting yetis and giant spiders and massive HellToads. And she had so many questions.

The last time anyone had heard from Alice's Granny Lydia was when she'd decided to head to the Amazon to hunt down the one monster that had truly terrified her. The same monster that had scared her so much it had caused a white stripe to appear in her hair – a stripe that would last generations! One that Alice shared, and which she liked to dye blue.

I'm talking about the **BÜÜÜÜG.**

Have you ever seen a **BÜÜÜÜG?**

I certainly hope not.

Anyway, Lydia never came back from that last trip and her real reason for going had been a secret up until Alice's discovery at Christmas.

The rest of the **PDF** thought that she'd probably been gobbled up or something, but no one wanted to say that in front of Alice as she was desperate to believe that her grandma was out there somewhere.

Mr Longblather had been told about poor old missing Lydia too, which is why he usually indulged Alice's questions, despite his protests at repeating himself. He pulled down a map of the Amazon he kept on a roller on the wall. Alice had started asking so often that it was just easier to have one always to hand. What Mr Longblather didn't know was that Alice kept asking questions to look for clues, in case her grandma was still around and able to help and she could somehow track her down.

'Fine,' Mr Longblather said. 'The Amazon rainforest is the world's largest rainforest, which you can find across Brazil, Peru, Colombia, Bolivia—'

'Not this again!' said Grenville Bile, grumpily. 'Why don't you just go find your nan if it means that much to you, Alice? You've got a bike.'

'Listen, prawn face,' said Alice, turning around with a face like thunder but remaining very calm. 'Maybe I will one day. Though probably not by bike. And I ask my questions because it's important to be *prepared*. And of course it means that much to me. It's *family*.'

She shot him a withering glance, but Grenville couldn't even spell withering so it was mostly wasted on him. Alice cracked her knuckles and decided to let it go.

'Yeah, it's family,' said Grenville, forgetting to be scared of Alice, even though you totally should. 'But you never even met her. You told us that she disappeared when your mum was a little girl.'

'She had her reasons,' said Alice, seething. 'Because Grandma Lydia was not someone who gives up. And neither am I.'

'Prove it,' said Grenville, who had learned to talk like this from watching old wrestling videos and had just decided that making Alice angry might be a way to distract Mr Longblather from trying to continue the lesson.

Alice leaned down and pulled an ancient-looking notebook out of her bag. It had old postcards and newspaper clippings poking from it and Hamish recognised it as Alice's grandma's travel diary. She never seemed to go anywhere without it lately.

'I'm looking for clues, Grenville, and do you know why? Because that's what she'd have done. Because she's part of me. And as this monster gets closer, we're all starting to realise how important family is, aren't we?'

Maybe this was Alice's way of coping with The News, thought Hamish. To focus on something else. To imagine an adventure she could control. But then she said something that stopped him in his tracks.

'That's the thing about family,' she said. 'They're always a part of us.'

Hamish shifted uncomfortably in his seat.

'Their *good* bits, and their *bad* bits, they *all* go into us,' she said, on a roll now. 'Our family makes us who we are.'

An image of Scarmarsh formed in Hamish's mind and he promptly tried to push it away, but he was starting to feel a bit sick.

'There's no getting away from it,' said Alice, opening the diary to a picture of Lydia. 'You can't hide from it. Whatever is in your blood, is *in your blood*.'

Hamish stood up and left the room.

5

DAYS UNTIL ARRIVAL:
YUP, STILL 5

'Hey, H! What's up?' said Buster, bounding over to Hamish in the playground at break. 'You just stood up and walked out! I was all like, "why's Hamish stood up and walked out?"'

'I was, um, feeling a bit sick,' said Hamish. 'What did Mr Longblather say?'

'He looked like he was going to get annoyed so we just asked him what trains were like when he was young.'

The rest of the **PDF** joined the boys in the playground.

'Right!' Clover said, sounding determined. 'Now that we finally have a break from "education", we can focus on the important stuff. What are we going to do about this monster? The rest of the country won't have anything to do with us until we sort this out! We've got to nip it in the butt!'

Hamish had heard they were planning to build an even bigger wall around Starkley in the next few days. Just to really send a message to the monster that while Starkley may be of interest to it, that was no reason to attack the rest of the country. Of course, some people were furious. What happened to everyone being in it together? But the new prime minister, Anna Tank-Topp, had been adamant. Starkley seemed to love monsters, and monsters seemed to love Starkley, she declared. What was sacrificing one little town if it saved thousands more? And if people wanted to stay there – even though they couldn't get as many sausages or sweeties – that was *their* problem!

All this just made people prouder to be living in brave, plucky Starkley right now. The Starkley Town Council flag flew proudly on roofs and in gardens.

Of course, secretly the kids knew their parents would be planning for the worst. Unless **Belasko** could come up with an amazing plan in the next five days, then they'd be forced to move. Buster would end up at his auntie's house in London. Clover's family would head for Suffolk. Venk had family in Scotland. Whatever happened, though, the **PDF** knew it was important not to lose sight of the present because it wasn't too late to stop the monster!

So far, the gang had three main plans of their own:

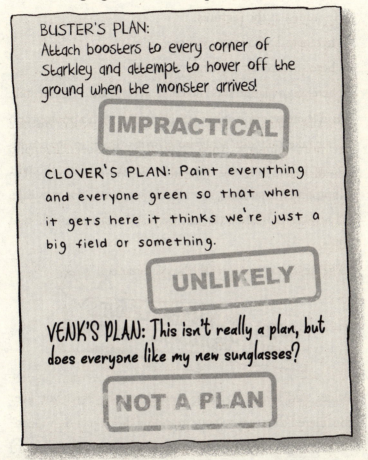

BUSTER'S PLAN:
Attach boosters to every corner of Starkley and attempt to hover off the ground when the monster arrives!

IMPRACTICAL

CLOVER'S PLAN: Paint everything and everyone green so that when it gets here it thinks we're just a big field or something.

UNLIKELY

VENK'S PLAN: This isn't really a plan, but does everyone like my new sunglasses?

NOT A PLAN

'Hmm,' said Hamish. 'Well, I'm not sure we've quite cracked it yet.'

'I wonder if Granny Lydia ever faced anything like this,' said Alice, leafing through the travel diary.

'Can I see?' said Elliot, and she handed it to him.

He smiled at the pictures.

There was Lydia in snowshoes.

There she was on top of a mountain.

There was a picture she'd taken of an elephant. A ticket stub.

And there was one of her travel reviews with a photograph of her taken outside a big hotel, with three ornate domes on top. Lydia had a curious expression on her face, thought Elliot. She was smiling, sure. But it was quite a forced smile.

'This was published the day before she disappeared,' said Alice.

The headline underneath the picture read:

HOTEL EMPANADA LEAVES PEOPLE MARVELLOUSLY ENTERTAINED!

'Alice,' said Buster, looking a bit sheepish. 'Have you ever considered that maybe your grandma didn't just disappear?'

Alice knew what Buster was going to say, because she'd thought about it herself.

'Sometimes people vanish on purpose,' he said, sadly. 'Sometimes . . . they might have a secret that makes them not want to be found.'

Hamish winced at the word secret. He hated hiding things from his best friends. The **PDF** always shared everything, but he was ashamed about his link to Scarmarsh and worried that if he did tell his pals they would react badly. What if they no longer trusted him, because how could you truly trust the nephew of the second most evil villain in the universe?

Or, worse, what if they *blamed* him?

Blamed him for everything. For the WorldStoppers, for the SpyTraps, maybe even for the monster making its way towards Starkley now? What if they were angry at him for how much everything had changed in their boring little town for the worse?

But, really, at the root of all Hamish's worries was the fact that he was *scared*. He didn't want to tell them just in case they were *right*.

'Uh, guys?' said Elliot, peering more closely at Lydia's diary. 'I think there might be more to Lydia's story than we thought.'

'What are you talking about?' asked Alice.

'I think I've found a clue,' said Elliot. 'A good one.'

'I've been through that book a thousand times,' said Alice. 'I think if there was a good clue I'd have found it by now.'

'What have you seen, El?' said Hamish, grateful for any distraction from his own thoughts.

'This article,' said Elliot. 'Look at it.'

'It's the last piece she ever wrote as a travel writer. Just as she was going into the Amazon.' Alice shrugged. 'What about it?'

'Does she really look happy in that photo?' said Elliot. 'Or, just under the surface, does she look scared? The strange smile? The bulging eyes? The sheen of sweat?'

'Maybe she'd just had a bad curry?' said Buster. 'Mmm, curry.'

But the closer they looked . . . yes. Perhaps the look of fear was indeed there, just under the surface.

'But that's not a clue,' continued Venk. 'A clue is like a fingerprint or a hidden message or something. Not a bad photo after a dodgy korma.'

'*Yes*, Venk,' said Elliot. 'So now look at the headline. . .'

They did.

Hotel Empanada Leaves People Marvellously Entertained!

Everyone looked blank.

So Elliot tapped at the H in Hotel.

And then the E in Empanada.

And then he moved his way along the sentence . . .

HOTEL
EMPANADA
LEAVES
PEOPLE
MARVELLOUSLY
ENTERTAINED!

'H. E. L. P. M. E.!' gasped Alice. 'Grandma Lydia must have known what was going to happen! She was asking for help because she knew it was a trap!'

'Oh,' said Elliot, wisely. 'It gets a *lot* more interesting than that . . .'

6

DAYS UNTIL ARRIVAL:
JUST OVER 4 (5)

'This is AMAZING!' yelled Alice, pounding down the street as her friends tried to keep up with her. **'This is INSANE!'**

Alice was pretty much the fastest runner in Starkley. Let's just say the others were not.

'Wait!' puffed Elliot. 'Shouldn't we discuss this?'

'YOU KIDS STAY SAFE!' yelled PC Wix, watching them run through the empty street. 'Make sure you're in by curfew tonight!'

'Shouldn't you be in school?' yelled Madame Cous Cous, polishing her window. The News had been bad for International World of Treats. Fewer people were coming to Starkley these days, and not much stock was getting in either. All Madame Cous Cous had to sell these days was Frinkley Fudge, and some Starkley Spiced Apple Slime, which was just some rotten apples she'd put pepper on.

Alice burst through the front door of her house and bounded upstairs, pausing once and once only to kiss her rabbit, Benny.

By the time the others had made it to her room, Alice was already coming back down the ladder to the loft carrying a small bag.

'Gonna need a decent bag,' she said.

'Wait,' said Hamish. 'What are you doing?'

'Isn't it obvious?' said Alice, starting to throw things in the bag. 'She might still be out there! We have to save Grandma Lydia. We have to go to the Amazon.'

'What?!' said Buster.

'Uh, that sounds pretty far away,' said Clover. 'And shouldn't we be concentrating on this sea monster? Like, that feels like it should be our next mission . . . I mean, it's not rocket salad.'

'Fine,' said Alice. 'You stay and deal with that. And maybe **Belasko** can take me to the Amazon.'

But everyone knew what their answer would be: we've

got our own problems right here in Starkley! There's a sea monster coming, Alice! We can't send a plane off to the Amazon to find someone's nana who disappeared into the ether decades ago and might not even still be alive! Where would you even start?!'

'You said the clue was more interesting than just the words, Elliot,' said Alice. 'Did you find something else?'

'Lydia is holding up a map in the photo,' said Elliot. 'Why would she do that? Unless it was to help show exactly where she was heading the next day?'

'Good thought,' said Venk.

'But this is even more intriguing,' said Elliot. 'Just like with the headline, if you take the first letter of each word in the opening sentence in the Hotel Empanada review, it spells out something too . . .'

ANY SEASON, KURIOUS FOREIGNERS OFTEN REALISE HOTELS ARE REALLY RATHER YUMMY!

'She spelled "curious" wrong,' said Venk. 'And, how can a hotel be "yummy"? Who's eating hotels?'

'To be fair, it must be pretty hard to hide clues while still conveying a good sense of the travel experience,' said Clover.

Alice worked it out. A . . . S . . . K . . .

'*Ask for Harry!*' she said. 'But where? How?'

'I guess at Hotel Empanada,' said Hamish. 'If it still exists. I mean, this was a long time ago, Alice.'

'Then that just means she's been waiting years for someone to help her. I know she's still out there, Hamish.'

Hamish could see the determination in his friend's eyes. But Alice couldn't go to the Amazon! It was on the other side of the world! They'd have to get, like, a bus, and a cab, and a train, and then probably walk for a bit, and then get a coach to the airport, and then get a plane, and then another plane, and then a bus, and a train . . . and that would be just to get out of Britain! Plus, Hamish only had about forty pounds saved up from Christmas, and he was pretty sure there was no way their parents would let them go to the Amazon on some crazy granny-hunt. Because what if it was all just a wild goose chase?

But he didn't want to discourage Alice, who was now packing monster books, a self-defence guide called *Kickin'*

Butt and a nut and pickle baguette.

'Hotel Empanada!' said Elliot, excited, pointing at some scribbled-down notes at the back of the travel diary. 'Lydia wrote down the phone number!'

'Great!' said Alice. 'So I can call it, ask for Harry, and see what happens.'

Hamish was secretly pretty sure that would be the end of it. The number would probably not even work. Whoever Harry was would have retired. But at least Alice would have tried and she could move on from thinking about Lydia.

Clover tossed her the home phone and Alice started to dial.

She put it on speakerphone and the kids gathered round.

A long, dull ringtone crackled into life.

BVVVVVVV.

The number worked!

BVVVVVVV.

But surely it wouldn't still be Hotel Empanada?

BVVVVVVV.

And surely Harry wouldn't be there?

BVVVVVVV.

And surely no one would ever have heard of Lydia?

BVVVVVVV.

This was going on a bit too long.

BVVVVV— 'Hello?'

The kids gasped. A voice. A young, male voice, with a slight accent.

'Hello,' said Alice. 'My name is Alice Shepherd and I'm looking for my grandma Lydia. Is Harry there?'

Silence.

Then...

'I'm logging the co-ordinates of your phone,' said the voice. 'Hotel Empanada is pleased to offer a shuttlebus service.'

And just before the line went dead, the voice uttered two more words.

'Be prepared.'

THE DREAM

Floating away from his friends, across the sea . . . the rain as hard as needles. And this time it was clearer than ever.

The strange grip so tight around his waist, it's hard to breathe . . .

He can hardly catch his breath as the wind whips around his face . . .

The clouds around him seem darker tonight. They shift and change rapidly, the cracks of thunder leave his ears ringing as he cascades through the air towards something . . .

But what?

Whatever it is can't be good. Why can't he have nicer dreams? Dreams where he dances around in a land of candy floss and chocolate rivers, skipping over rainbows while being chased by a friendly unicorn called Dumpling?

But no. This is his dream. As real as anything you're looking at now.

A world so cold and dark and wet.

Hamish feels hopeless as he loses all sight of where he could possibly be.

Now the grip around his waist loosens.

He stops perfectly still in the air . . .

The waves somewhere down beneath him crash and roll. Lightning crackles through the air. Wind and untameable electricity prickle his skin.

The swirling clouds begin to take a different form altogether.

Something takes shape in front of him . . .

7

DAYS UNTIL ARRIVAL: 4!

When Hamish got up for breakfast the next day, he thought immediately about Alice. What kind of hotel would send a bus all the way from the Amazon to Starkley? They were obviously mad. Maybe they thought Alice had been making a prank call. Plus, buses were notoriously slow. It would take months to arrive! And how was it going to get over the ocean?!

There were more pressing issues at hand, in any case.

As he sat down at the breakfast table, Hamish could hear his dad talking to some other people in his study. Hamish used every opportunity he could to listen into his dad's discussions. It was all useful intel to pass on to the **PDF**. In an ideal world, what Hamish really craved was the chance to join his dad on a mission. Or to have his dad join him on one. And not a rubbish mission either, like one where you sit in a van for six hours and stare at a house. But a cool mission. One where the very fate of the world would rest on the actions of Angus

Ellerby and his boy. Anyway, he could hear they were talking about the monster.

'That's if it even is a monster!' one person was saying. 'We don't know for certain! We just know something is coming and that it seems to be growing. Maybe it's something nice!'

'Like what?' a lady barked.

'Like . . . a lovely big kitten?' the man tried.

Hamish's dad had also been keeping him pretty up-to-date on all the news. The difference was, when he talked to Hamish he would say things like, 'It's probably nothing to worry about.' And when he talked to other grown-ups he sounded very worried indeed. But he shared whatever he could with Hamish because, as he liked to remind him, Hamish was a junior **Belasko** agent, after all. And his dad loved hearing Hamish's ideas, because someone had once told him that 'kids think differently'.

Hamish had barely shovelled some cornflakes into his mouth when outside, the siren began to wail. Then the Central Speaker began to honk.

'Oh, not again!' said his mum, walking in with a teetering pile of paperwork. Emails and letters had been piling up in the Complaints Department of Starkley Town Council, because people had quite a lot to moan about these days. Like the power cuts. And the fact the heating didn't work sometimes. And the way the taps would only trickle most mornings. And of course the constant honking of the Central Speaker, which really annoyed the woman who lived right opposite it. She said it was like having a mad opera singer shouting randomly in your garden all day.

Dad burst out of his study as the Central Speaker continued honking.

'This is not a drill!' he was shouting into his walkie-talkie, and outside, all the lamp posts began flashing blue and red. **'A UFO has been spotted heading to Starkley – and fast!'**

A UFO?

Now, Hamish knew not to get carried away. UFO just meant an unidentified flying object. I mean, a bird is a UFO until you've identified that it's a bird. If you shot your teacher out of a cannon, they'd be a UFO. Or at least a **UFT**.

Oh my gosh. Imagine a whole sky filled with UFTs. You'd never have anywhere to hide!

'Where's it heading?' said Dad, and the crackly response came back.

Too crackly.

'Where?' he said, grimacing, because we all think that if we grimace we can suddenly hear better for some reason.

But Hamish had heard just enough to work it out.

He leapt out of his seat to run for the door and grab his bike. He was absolutely certain the crackly voice had said the word 'Viola'.

As he pedalled through Starkley, Hamish saw **Belasko** agents jumping into trucks all over the place. There was blind panic. They were bumping into each other, dropping their car keys, slapping each other out of the way so they could be the one to drive. Was the UFO the start of another invasion of some kind? Did it have anything to do with the slow-moving sea monster? They still had four days to come up with a plan, didn't they?!

Hamish reached Viola Road, skidding to a halt on the tarmac which was slick from rain.

He looked up in disbelief.

There was a FLASH of light and he was hit by a blast of hot air. He shielded his eyes and stared at the ground. Beneath him, the wet road dried almost instantly as water and puddles were swept away by something from above.

There were fumes in the air, and the noise of . . . what was that?

A chopper? A jet plane?

Hamish felt tiny against its power and ear-blistering racket.

'Hamish!'

A tiny voice almost cut through the roar of the engine. Hamish looked up and, through the wobbly air from the fumes and a sky full of dust and old Epic Soda cans and plastic bottles of Anonymous Sauce that had been blown from the bins, he could just make out Alice standing outside her front gate. She was pointing upwards excitedly.

Hamish unshielded his eyes and saw that, above them both, some kind of flying machine was lowering itself slowly on to the street.

It was boxy, and NOISY, and long, with three landing skis that now juddered from the base. On the side was some kind of logo. A pair of eyes and a scowl and the letters MP.

MP?

Military Police?

Member of Parliament?

Mucky Pups?

The machine didn't look slick or particularly cool – it looked almost home-made, and dented, and like a scrappy hunk of clunkering steel. You could see all the places it had been mended too, with metal plates hammered over dents and holes. Hamish squinted to see if he could make out who was flying it. There were two shapes in the front window as it turned to make its final landing and slow its engines.

'Hotel shuttlebus!' mouthed Alice, looking delighted. Her eyes were shining with excitement. But Hamish wasn't so sure. He ran to Alice protectively, which was nice, though entirely unnecessary, as Alice was the one with all the kung-fu books.

Now landed, a great burst of white steam rolled over the ground like fallen clouds – and a door fell open. The kids held their breath. **Belasko** agents were arriving, their cars coming to a halt behind the Alice and Hamish.

But Alice didn't want the grown-ups to take over. This was *her* house; *her* street. She stepped forward.

'Hello?' she tried. 'I'm Alice Shepherd! And this is my friend, Hamish Ellerby!'

From the smoke, a figure emerged.

A kid!

Maybe twelve years old and wearing some kind of dark blue boiler suit – like a plumber! – with that same 'MP' logo on his chest, and yellow stripes down each arm and leg.

'They call me Kit!' he said confidently and with a light accent. 'Kit Alexander Lopez. And I'm here to pick you up so we can look for your grandmamma.'

This was not the way people normally introduced themselves. And who says 'grandmamma'? Alice was intrigued.

'Why do you want to help me look for my Grandma Lydia?' she said, in awe, because this kid was pretty cool. 'Who are you exactly?'

'I literally just said I was Kit Alexander Lopez,' said Kit Alexander Lopez, who had indeed literally just said he was Kit Alexander Lopez.

Then he smiled and pointed at the logo on the plane.

'Monster Patrol,' he said, proudly. He looked around at the tall security fences and warning signs. 'What in the name of *Julio* is happening here?!'

Alice was a little intimidated by this guy. He was so sure of himself . . . and also weird.

'WAIT!'

Hamish spun round to see his dad. Angus Ellerby strode up the street with some of the other **Belasko** agents. 'Monster Patrol? You guys wound up years ago! You don't exist!'

'Oh, we *exist*, mister sir,' said Kit. 'But we operate in – how you say – the shadows. And what I mean by that is we operate in secret, not that we hide behind curtains.'

'Okay,' said Hamish's dad.

'Also, yes, maybe we are fewer in number than in the old days. And we might have a smaller budget. But we're here. We're *dedicado*. And we're PREPARED.'

'**Right!**' shouted Alice, clapping her hands together, totally convinced. 'Enough light chit-chat! Let's go, Hamish!' She started to clamber onboard the plane.

'Wait,' said Hamish. 'What?'

'Let's go!' said Alice. 'They sent a shuttle! Kit's here. Let's go find my grandma!'

'We can't just . . . *go*,' said Hamish, who was always up for adventure and totally got how important it was to always try and save the world, but was also still quite sensible. 'You need to ring your mum at work and ask her! And there's a monster coming! And we've got school tomorrow!'

'Kit,' said Dad. 'How many of you are there left in Monster Patrol?'

'Well, we are having to operate under the radar, *señor*,' said Kit. 'And that makes advertising for vacancies a little tricky.'

'**Belasko** used to work closely with Monster Patrol

many years ago,' said Dad, looking at Hamish. 'It was before I joined. Before Monster Patrol changed the way it did. But the story was that Lydia disappeared and **Belasko** presumed she passed away.'

Alice's face fell and Hamish's dad winced realising how insensitive that sounded.

'You knew about my grandma?' she said. 'Why didn't you tell me that? Why did no one tell me about Monster Patrol?'

She was interrupted by Kit.

'Mister dad, we think Lydia is alive. Only problem is, we don't know where.'

'I *knew* she was alive!' said Alice, her heart leaping.

'All we found when she disappeared was a single boot in the jungle. Her travel diary was lost, and we ran out of clues,' Kit continued. 'But then, Alice, you called and asked for "Harry" – the secret Monster Patrol password. So we wondered who you were and how you could have got that information. And we realised you must have seen a clue in the diary. And no matter how hopeless something may seem, you must never ignore a clue. So **LET'S GO!'**

Hamish's eyes widened as Kit yelled. This kid was a real

bellower. Hamish looked at Alice. She was bright-eyed and keen to go.

'I've got the diary right here!' she said.

'**Then we GO!**' Kit said, in a booming voice. He signalled through the window at his co-pilot and the plane's engines fired up. A great rattling, shaky noise that blew the dust up from the street and wobbled the lamp posts.

'Alice!' came a desperate, pleading voice. 'Wait!'

'What is it, Grenville?' Alice said kindly.

He was looking up at her, with big round eyes. She reckoned she knew exactly what this was. Yes, they had their differences, but Grenville must suddenly be proud she was finally getting the chance to find her grandma, and he was clearly about to say something very touching.

He looked up at her with two pleading eyes.

'Can you bring me back a prawn burrito?' he said.

Oh.

'Dad,' said Hamish, ignoring this because he'd had an idea. An idea that would not only mean he could protect his friend, but help Starkley too. 'What if Lydia could be useful?'

'Useful?' said Dad.

'To us. To Starkley. With her particular set of skills . . .'

Dad's eyes widened.

'Kit!' he shouted. 'If Lydia is still out there, *find* her. Tell her Starkley needs her help. Tell her there's something coming – something BIG – and we don't know how to stop it.'

'Come on, Hamish!' shouted Alice, over the din of the engines. 'I can hardly do this without you, can I? **We're a team!'**

Hamish swallowed. This was happening a bit too quickly.

'You don't have to go, pal,' his dad told him. 'This is Alice's mission. She's got Kit to help her. And Monster Patrol don't exactly do things the **Belasko** way. Also, your mum will go mad if I let you go off to the Amazon on a school day.'

There was a time when Hamish would have been cross with his dad for trying to stop him going on an adventure, but Hamish knew why his dad was saying this. He was doing his job as a dad and protecting his son.

'Why don't you come with us, Dad?' said Hamish, which was another way of saying he was going anyway. 'It'd be fun. Me and you off on a mission together.'

And do you know what? Hamish's dad almost believed that was a good idea. Like, for a second he forgot his responsibilities. No, for like a microsecond. No, for like a fifth of a microsecond.

But no matter how long that pause was, it wasn't enough.

He couldn't leave Starkley when a sea monster was on its way.

Hamish understood, just from the look on his dad's face. And he knew he had a job to do too. With only four days to go until the experts expected the sea monster, maybe Hamish had found a glimmer of hope.

'Tell the rest of the **PDF** to get to HQ,' Hamish said. 'We'll ring Garage 5 when we get there.'

'Get where?' said Dad.

'To Hotel Empanada,' said Hamish. 'Alice needs me. And I think Starkley needs Lydia if we have any chance against whatever monster is coming our way.'

Hamish's dad nodded his head.

'If she's still alive, and you can save Alice's grandma,' he said, 'maybe Alice's grandma can save us.'

And Hamish's dad smiled with pride, because he knew what was coming next.

Hamish turned and ran for the shuttle.

8

DAYS UNTIL ARRIVAL:
STILL 4

'*Bienvenido* to the Astral Plane,' said Kit, welcoming them, and ka-shunking the steel door shut before putting one finger in the air. 'Now. I'm about to introduce you to my co-pilot. It's SUPER-important that you don't freak out.'

Hamish and Alice glanced at each other. That didn't seem like a very good sentence to hear. Like someone saying: 'My dad has made you his special fishcakes. Try not to vomit after eating one.' Or, 'Here, I got you a present! Hopefully it won't explode yet!'

But there was something about Kit they trusted. He seemed no-nonsense. Very in control. He seemed like a kid with a plan.

'Smasha, let's rock,' yelled Kit, leading Alice and Hamish towards the cockpit, past rows of wooden drawers and cabinets . . .

Wait.

WHAT THE HECK WAS THAT AT THE FRONT
OF THE SHIP?

'Alice, Hamish . . . meet Smasha.'

The strange figure turned around in its chair and Hamish
and Alice did their best not to freak out, which was hard,
because . . .

WHAT THE HECK WAS THAT?!

He was tall.

That's if he was a he.

And he was furry. Not the way your mad uncle Jonno is

furry. This was actual fur.

Smasha seemed to have the body of a fox, with great tufts of hair buffling out of his boiler suit.

But, and this was the really weird bit . . .

He seemed to have the *head* . . .

Of . . .

A puffer fish!

Two big eyes! A couple of nostrils! Four little teeth!

The weird-looking creature licked his fox fingers and pointed at Alice and Hamish, then got back to pressing buttons on the dashboard.

'Smasha is my Familiar,' said Kit, taking the co-pilot seat and beckoning the others to sit down in the chairs behind him. 'He's what you call a Puffox.'

TYPE: PUFFOX

DESCRIPTION: Head of a puffer fish, body of a fox.

TEETH: Four. Who needs more?

SKILLS: When threatened, Smasha can inflate his own head to three times its original size. Poisonous needles fly from it. He is Fast! Cunning! Agile! Unable to chew very well!

LEVEL OF MONSTERING: Generally friendly. Loyal. The Puffox makes a great Familiar for any young Monster Patroller!

'Uh, what *is* a Familiar?' said Hamish, trying to sound as un-weirded-out as possible. 'I thought Monster Patrol would probably have a sort of *anti*-monster policy?'

Kit spun his chair round so he could talk to them properly. He clapped twice inexplicably – he seemed to have a lot of pent-up energy, this kid – then leaned forward.

'Monster Patrol was set up by two ace scientists who realised they had to operate in total secrecy if they were to protect the world.'

Ooh. This sounded good. And the way Kit spoke made it sound cool and fashionable.

'Who were they?' asked Alice, already totally fascinated.

'YOUR grandmamma,' said Kit. 'And MINE.'

Alice slapped Hamish's arm, delighted. Then Kit slapped Alice's arm, delighted. Grandma Lydia wasn't just *in* Monster Patrol. She *started* it!

Monster Patrol had a simple mission: to record any and all monster activity here on Earth, keep it under control and make everyone believe it was all just legend.

That's why you believe they're just legends, isn't it?

The Loch Ness Monster? Just a legend, you say!

Yetis? Spider-whales? Sea serpents? Just legends, surely!

Well, that's because Monster Patrol *convinced* you of that, you big simpleton.

But don't worry. It's for the best. Because there are SO MANY others you should count yourself lucky you don't know about . . .

TYPE: SNALLYGASTER

DESCRIPTION: All wings and claws and a big eye in the middle of its forehead! Makes a sound like a passing high-speed train! Half-reptile, half-bird, all monster!

LEVEL OF MONSTERING: Ghastly. Though mainly woodland-based, so if you see a tree – run!

> TYPE: THE GLAWACKUS
>
> DESCRIPTION: The terror of lumberjacks! Pounds through the forests. Blind, but uses smell and soundwaves – so make sure you use deodorant and keep quiet!
>
> LEVEL OF MONSTERING: Total. Though probably a bit more dangerous if you're a lumberjack. (Are you?)

> TYPE: WENDIGOS
>
> DESCRIPTION: Thin, bony and grey, like an angry teacher near retirement! The more it eats, the hungrier it becomes. Furious, unsatisfied and *hangry*! Pelts through the fields, faster than a puma! Faster than a puma with its bum on fire!
>
> LEVEL OF MONSTERING: Huge. Famed for its gluttony and greed. Make sure you don't see one at lunchtime! And that you're not dressed up as a sandwich or wearing your kebab trousers again!

And there were so many others. Moth-men. Stinkles. Thorpeness Crabbers. The Lala Boo. Kevin Webster.

And these were monsters that represented one word, said Kit as he explained it all to Hamish and Alice, their eyes full of wonder and fear. 'That one word is chaos! And you can't have all this chaos everywhere. It's waaay too chaotic!'

Lydia and Luciana had written a proposal to the local council in order to try and receive a small business loan to set up Monster Patrol.

DEAR THE BANK,

MONSTERS ARE CONFUSING TO NORMAL PEOPLE, WITH THEIR SANDWICHES FOR LUNCH AND THEIR POST OFFICE QUEUES AND TELEVISION PROGRAMMES ETC. MOST PEOPLE CAN'T HANDLE THE THOUGHT OF MONSTERS, BECAUSE MONSTERS DON'T OBEY THE LAWS OF NATURE.

BECAUSE WHAT ARE THEY . . . ? ARE THEY OF THIS WORLD, OR ANOTHER . . . ?

OOH, **NOW** YOU'RE INTRIGUED, AREN'T YOU? ANYWAY, WE NEED SOME MONEY FOR STATIONERY ETC.

Thankfully, the bank was owned by **Belasko**.

'So Monster Patrol was funded by Belasko?' asked Hamish. 'Then why aren't they still a part of it?'

'There were a few . . . disagreements on our approach,' said Kit. 'The things we believe.'

'Tell me more about Lydia!' said Alice.

'Once they got themselves stuck in,' said Kit, 'our grandmammas would convince the monsters that their only chance of survival was to hide away, deep in forests and jungles and, and never come out once more. This did two things. It protected people from monsters, and it protected monsters from people. Because, as I'm sure you know, not all monsters are bad.'

Hamish did not look convinced and was starting to see why **Belasko** might have had a few problems with Monster Patrol. I mean, sure, he'd met a friendly Venus SpyTrap once, but generally his experiences with monsters had been anything but good. In fact they'd been *monstrous*! One of them had even once stuck its finger up his nose!

Alice on the other hand thought back to a moment in her own life, not too long ago. She had met a monster on Christmas Eve – a young Terrible – and the two of them had found some common ground.

'I can believe they're not all bad,' she said, smiling at Kit.

Hamish stared at her, feeling a tinge of jealousy at how interested she seemed in Kit's words. Had she totally forgotten about all the problems monsters had caused them in the past? All the badness they brought to the world? Alice was a little too keen on this whole Monster Patrol thing for his liking.

'The fact is, we need some monsters,' said Kit.

'I'm not sure *that's* true,' began Hamish.

'No! Hamish – they are a hidden part of our ecosystem. One **MegaWorm** can fertilise fifteen fields in a minute. And, did you know the **Ultra-bee** can pollinate an entire orchard without even trying? Sure, it's got a temper. And one heck of a stinger. But it's important and helpful, too.'

'But what if the monsters wouldn't hide like our grandmas told them to?' said Alice, impressed. 'What if they weren't useful, they were just bad?'

'If the time came to *fight*,' said Kit, 'Monster Patrol knew exactly how to dispose of any huge and unwilling baddies. Because can you imagine the panic it would cause if they suddenly started attacking towns?'

Hamish raised his eyebrows. Yes, he could imagine that very well. Because in just four days it was literally about to happen once again in Starkley!

'Monster Patrol knew all the best ways of capturing them, and then they would take them to **Belasko**, who'd fly them to some other planet somewhere and let them roam free.

'We set up many offices and Lydia used her cover as a travel writer to interview the best and the brightest monster hunters, wherever they might live.'

'Cool!' said Alice.

'Monster Patrol offices were often hidden in plain sight,' Kit continued. 'An old post office here. An abandoned cinema there.'

'A hotel in the Amazon?' said Alice, and Kit smiled a *si*.

'If rumours of a Cactus Cat in Caracas came up, Monster Patrol was on it. If someone saw an Amorak Wolf pounding heavily through the Arctic Tundra, Monster Patrol would have fired up their *Snowgo*! snowmobiles and chased it through the ice.'

Alice's eyes widened even further at Kit's words. She couldn't believe that her grandma had led such an exciting life!

'Then Lydia had disappeared,' Kit said, sadly. 'My grandmamma Luciana couldn't do all the work by herself. They had been such a *team*, a *dúo*. And with one half totally vanished, Monster Patrol started to close its offices.

'Even then the bad monsters mostly stayed hidden because they feared my grandmamma still, but, as she grew older, she realised that if Monster Patrol was to have any chance of survival and keep the world safe, then she would have to find the next generation to carry on the work, that Monster Patrol needed to strengthen itself again,' said Kit. 'My grandmamma knew she was . . . not long for this world and became more and more worried that the truly evil monsters would feel safer with her gone and start to reappear again.'

A moment of sadness flashed across Kit's eyes. He dismissed it immediately.

'She taught me from the age of four what to do. And by the time I was ten . . . well, I was alone. But she had planned for that. One of her last decisions was the most important thing about the all-new Monster Patrol,' he said. 'She hatched a plan, to bring in Familiars.

Each MP team would be a kid and a pretty nice and cool monster who wanted to help make sure that the truth about monsters remained a secret too.'

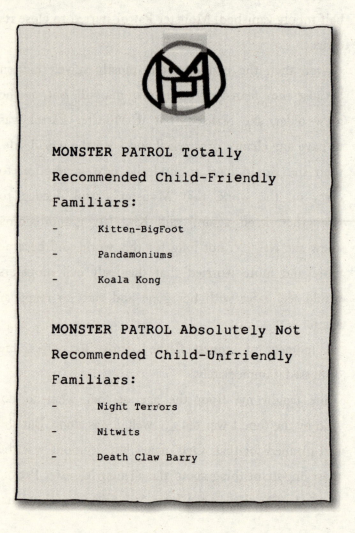

MONSTER PATROL Totally
Recommended Child-Friendly
Familiars:

-    Kitten-BigFoot

-    Pandamoniums

-    Koala Kong

MONSTER PATROL Absolutely Not
Recommended Child-Unfriendly
Familiars:

-    Night Terrors

-    Nitwits

-    Death Claw Barry

'Kids and monsters?!' said Hamish in shock. 'That's usually a dreadful combination!'

Hamish was right. Kids *and* monsters? Madness! But Luciana was smart. She knew that it was a risk, but she also knew that there was something that made kids special. She'd studied Kit when he was just a toddler. The way he'd solve a puzzle or do a jigsaw. The questions he'd ask. Kids, she decided, just think differently.

'Grown-ups suddenly get much more scared of things when they become the grown-ups,' said Kit, with great certainty. 'They see danger everywhere. "*Argh!* A bike! *Eek!* A fly! *Ooh!* A loud noise!" Especially when they become parents.'

Hamish thought of his mum. It was definitely true of her. But then he felt bad because, after all, his mum was one of the brave parents, staying in Starkley for as long as possible, despite the imminent monster attack. Because she thought it was the right thing to do and she trusted they'd find a way out of danger . . . somehow.

'When you're a kid,' said Kit, 'you take more risks *now*, and imagine the consequences *later*. And you think differently, so can find solutions to problems that grown-ups can't see. Kids are fearless and smart. That's a winning combination when it comes to fighting monsters!'

Alice smiled. That was exactly what the **PDF** was all about too, and had been since day one. Even Hamish had to grudgingly agree and put his jealousy to one side.

'So, we can hook up with the rest of Monster Patrol, right?' said Hamish. 'All these kids and their Familiars? Get a whole gang together! An army! Find Alice's nan and then all of us race back to Starkley and stop the sea monster!'

Smasha glanced at Kit knowingly.

'Er, well, I wouldn't say we're an army exactly . . .' said Kit.

'How many of you are there?' said Hamish.

Hamish could see that Kit was wondering how to put it.

'There are,' said Kit, slowly ... 'two.'

'Two?' said Hamish. 'Two teams?'

'Uh, no,' said Kit. 'Just two. Just me and Smasha.'

'What do you mean? What *happened* to all the Monster Patrol teams?!' said Alice.

'I said my grandmamma hatched a plan for Monster Patrol. I did not say she lived long enough to see it through. But *I* will. My grandmamma left me Smasha. Together we are Monster Patrol, and one day we will be many!'

Hamish nodded. He had to respect Kit's determination, even if he had found him a little cocky to start with.

'Well, *we're* here now too,' said Alice. 'So what's the plan?'

'Smasha,' said Kit, smiling coolly, and strapping himself in. 'Hit it.'

Smasha hit accelerate and the Astral Plane **BOOOOMED** through the sky.

9

DAYS UNTIL ARRIVAL: 5-1
(So...4)

'**Fantastico!**' shouted Kit, when the ship had been cruising high, high above the clouds for almost an hour. 'Take the wheel, Smasha!'

Kit turned to Alice, who was fixing an ALWAYS BE PREPARED badge to her top, almost as a way of reminding herself.

'Will you show me Lydia's travel diary?'

Alice fished it from her bag and handed it to him. Kit held it as if he was holding the most precious object imaginable. Alice turned, and stopped in her tracks. There were photos of her grandma on the wall, living a life she'd never imagined. Darting through jungles, laughing onboard ships, driving big jeeps. They were incredible to her, and she gasped. But she also felt a weight on her shoulders. Could she live up to her grandma's legacy? Maybe by rescuing her, she would.

Hamish looked around, just as stunned. He'd spent most of the journey taking in the walls of the ship. Right down one whole side was a *wunderkammer* – that's a German word that sort of means 'cabinet of wonders' – and inside were all manner of rare souvenirs and important historical objects. Hamish stood up and trailed his finger across the words that had been chiselled on to the various wooden drawers.

He paused on one of the drawers. 'What's a "yokai"?' he asked Kit.

'Japanese pond-dweller,' said Kit, slowly turning the pages of the diary as he searched for something. 'It looks like some old tadpole. Great manners, but attacks UNEXPECTEDLY!'

He made a face which would have been frightening, if it hadn't looked like some old tadpole.

Hamish opened a drawer at random. Inside was a giant tooth.

'A Chinese Dragon tooth?' read Hamish, as Alice joined him and opened a drawer of her own.

'That's a Unicorn tusk, Alice,' said Kit. 'Sharpest tusk that exists. It can cut through *diamantes*.'

This was incredible. I mean, Hamish and Alice had seen some strange things over the last year, but even so, they'd never really considered that maybe dragons and unicorns were real and that their tusks could cut through *diamonds*!

'Wait – unicorns don't have tusks,' said Alice, who'd never considered a unicorn to be a monster.

'Oh, don't they? And I suppose they don't breathe fire either?' said Kit, who was not used to being questioned on his knowledge of monsters.

'What about this one?' said Hamish, holding up a strange-looking green object.

'Gremlin claw,' said Kit, and Hamish dropped it immediately. 'Of course, those drawers are very much a *grandmamma* system. All handwritten notes and filing in alphabeticals. I'm working on modernising things. Got my own BDNA system.'

'BDNA?' said Hamish.

'Beast DNA . . . I take samples from any monster I find and add them to a big database I'm creating. Eventually we'll know what kind of monster almost anything is.'

'That's smart!' said Hamish. 'Our friend Elliot would freak! How do you do it?'

'Well, I have to get close enough to shove a cotton stick in the monster's cheek and then swipe. *You* try doing that with a Giant HellToad that's gone crazy on terrorberries!'

Hamish and Alice glanced at each other. That was not a job either of them fancied.

'Got any sea monsters on that database?' asked Hamish. 'We could do with some ideas on how to get rid of those!'

'It does not surprise me that you're facing a sea monster,' said Kit. 'Most monsters are aquatic nowadays. The oceans cover two thirds of Earth. It's funny, humans always think this is "our" planet, but we forget that most of it is water and none of us have gills!'

Everyone looked at Smasha.

'No offence, *camarada*,' said Kit, and Smasha made a noise that sounded like 'Harrumph'.

Kit stopped as he found the newspaper cutting of Lydia at the Hotel Empanada.

'Oh!' said Hamish, remembering. 'Elliot thought the map Lydia's holding here might be a clue. Do you recognise it?'

Kit's eyes widened. He grabbed a bottle of water and held it in front of the map like a magnifying glass. 'Interesting!'

'Why?' said Alice.

'We did not search the area on the map,' said Kit. 'We found Lydia's boot about a mile away from the hotel. That was the way she seemed to be heading. But maybe something knocked her off course as she searched for the BÜÜÜÜG?'

'Uh, what's a BÜÜÜÜG?' said Hamish, and this was a question he really did not want to know the answer to.

'I know about the BÜÜÜÜG,' said Alice, happy she could show off some monster knowledge in front of Kit. 'It's a sort of giant fly-worm-beetle-bug that's all horned and taloned and toothed! And the worst thing about it is how patient it is! It'll grab its prey and wait for years until it becomes *just* tasty enough to eat! Grandma Lydia came up against it once before and it nearly made her give up monster hunting! She was so frightened she got an instant white stripe in her hair!'

'Oh, it is a fearsome beast,' agreed Kit. 'Let me attempt to piece this together using only my mind . . .'

LYDIA MADE HER WAY DEEP INTO THE JUNGLE, HACKING WILDLY AT THE VINES TO TRY AND FIND THE BÜÜÜÜG . . .

BUT BEFORE SHE GOT THERE, SHE ENCOUNTERED SOMETHING UTTERLY GHASTLY THAT GRABBED HER AND TOOK HER WILDLY OFF COURSE!

LOST IN THE JUNGLE, WITH NO SUPPLIES, AND COMPLETELY ALONE, AND WITH ONLY ONE BOOT, SHE HAD TO FIND SHELTER . . .

WHICH IS WHEN, WHILE SLEEPING, THE BÜÜÜÜG SURPRISED HER AND TOOK HER TO ITS LAIR! AAAAAARRRGH!

'How do you know all that?' said Alice, impressed yet mildly disturbed.

'I do *not* know all that,' said Kit. 'But I will know more when I've studied this diary and map properly. Lydia must have sent your mother the travel diary the day she set off to find the BÜÜÜÜG. Something must have made her think she needed to post the diary somewhere safe. She published the article when she knew where she was going, stuck it in the diary, and sent it off to your mother.'

'But why would she send it?' said Alice.

'Perhaps she realised she was being followed and she panicked,' said Kit. 'Maybe she only suspected it. But we think she was followed.'

'By who?' said Hamish.

'The Superiors,' said Kit. 'When they first had their eyes on Earth, they did not think the idea of fewer monsters was in their interests. And they certainly didn't want people around who were good at battling them. Of course, since then other enemies have come. Enemies every bit as powerful, who have learnt from the Superiors and also want to make Earth theirs.'

Hamish knew who that sounded like. But didn't want to say anything or even think about it. He told himself he couldn't tell Kit anyway, because then Kit might not trust him. He might think Hamish was a spy.

'I can't believe it,' said Alice, looking at the diary. 'It's just been in our attic for years.'

'You found it for a reason,' Hamish told her. 'But what about *your* grandma, Kit? Tell us about her.'

Kit picked up a photo from the cabinet of wonders. In it, Lydia was wearing a snowsuit, and Luciana wore a long tweed dress and boots.

'My grandmamma was a little different from Lydia. Different skills. A little more . . . experimental.'

Hamish could tell from the pictures on the wall of the plane that, despite their differences, Lydia and Luciana must have been a crack team.

There was Lydia, all action, charging into situations and taking control. Barking orders at monsters and leaping around.

And there was Luciana Lopez – calmer, studying the creatures, understanding them, and using whatever tricks she had up her to sleeve to solve the problem.

'She was quite an . . . *unusual* . . . woman,' said Kit. 'She started off as a science teacher. But the more she studied voodoo and hoodoo, the more she thought it could be useful. She thought maybe they would respond to . . . well, to magic.'

Hamish frowned. Magic?

Hmmm. Hamish suspected this might be why Monster Patrol and **Belasko** had gone their separate ways. **Belasko** tended not to put its faith in the unknown.

But Luciana had studied it all. Mayan magic. Far Eastern magic. Latin American magic. Close-up magic. Coin tricks. That one where you pretend your thumb is someone's nose. Any and all the magic she could.

'Uh, one thing I'd like to say,' said Alice. 'I mean, I *love* Monster Patrol and everything, but magic isn't real.'

'People have different opinions,' said Kit, shifting uncomfortably in his seat. 'Anyway, they started Monster Patrol as a way to help the world. And sometimes helping the world is the best way to make an enemy—'

And then Smasha started to get excited. Because he could see that far down below, they were running out of ocean, and about to whizz over land.

They were getting closer to Hotel Empanada.

10

DAYS UNTIL ARRIVAL: 4, THOUGH REMEMBER TO ALLOW FOR A SLIGHT TIME DIFFERENCE ON ACCOUNT OF FOREIGN TRAVEL

'Okay, I'm ready,' said Alice, leaping from the machine. 'Let's get deep into the jungle and kick some BUUUUG butt!'

She struck a karate pose and jumped about, getting to know her environment. It was mainly trees and a small frog. But the sounds of the jungle were everywhere.

The chirrup of tree crickets. The calls of the Bare-Throated Bellbirds.

'I took the liberty of preparing a few items before we came to collect you,' said Kit, handing them both Monster Patrol backpacks and jumping out. 'I hope you both like cactus sandwiches, cactus tea and cactus sugar?'

'Ooh, um, lovely,' said Hamish, who had been very well brought up but did not, in fact, think cacti belonged in sandwiches. He peeked inside. There were cactus tea bags, and cactus sugar lumps . . . oh, and one green banana. His tummy rumbled. Maybe if they sorted all this out, Starkley would have chips again.

Hamish clambered from the shuttle and looked up at Hotel Empanada. It was definitely the place from the newspaper article. But it really didn't look like a proper hotel any more. The paint was peeling, the many arched windows were boarded up, and the sign was hanging loose. The three strange domes at the top of the hotel – which had once been golden – were green now, and covered in vines.

And there didn't seem to be any other guests. Mind you, who'd stay here? Hamish knew they were somewhere between Ecuador and Peru, but that didn't really mean much to him, because he didn't really know where Ecuador and Peru were. The shuttle bus had flown for ages over miles and miles and miles of thick green forest so there was nothing much around. No other buildings. No shops. No tourist sights. It was a very strange place to start a hotel. But then, you even get hotels in Swindon these days.

'*Hola*,' said a strange frog man carrying a tea tray and wearing an ill-fitting suit.

'*Hola*,' replied Hamish, yawning. He was tired.

WAIT! WHY WAS THERE A STRANGE TALKING FROG MAN WITH A TRAY?

'That's Brendon,' said Kit. 'He looks after the hotel. Keeps people away. A very lonely job. He keeps asking me to get him a pet. Anyway, he stops anyone snooping around Monster Patrol HQ.'

'How does he do that?' asked Hamish.

Brendon unfurled an enormous, three-metre-long tongue and cracked it back into his mouth, like a whip. Hamish reckoned that was probably how.

'Right, come on, I want to get out there,' said Alice, still in a karate stance. 'What's the plan?'

'And, just out of interest . . . what are the dangers we should know about?' said Hamish. 'I mean, we're sort of in the middle of the jungle, right? I mean, if even *Lydia* needed help, shouldn't we be more prepared? Alice says we should *always* be prepared.'

Kit started to laugh.

'ABP!' he said.

'Huh?' said Alice.

'Always Be Prepared,' he said. 'That's the Monster Patrol slogan! But don't worry. Everyone thinks the jungle is so dangerous. But really it's fine. I mean, there are the spiders . . .'

'Spiders,' said Hamish, prickling with sweat. 'Sure.'

'And of course the rattlesnakes and the boa constrictors, those are quite bad.'

'Mm-hmm,' said Hamish, feeling queasy.

'There are the bullet ants. The red-bellied piranhas, the electric eels, and the poison darts frog. And the jaguars, alligators, giant otters and the hungry harpy eagle.'

'Okay,' said Hamish, a little pale now. 'Good to know.'

'And the wildfires, the dangerous river currents, the flash

floods, the falling trees, the lightning storms and the mud slides.'

'Cool,' said Alice, desperate to get started. 'But apart from that . . .'

'Well, apart from that, the chance of jungle sickness, fever, malaria, dehydration and some *serious* tummy trouble.'

'Uh-huh, tummy trouble, okay,' said Hamish. 'But that's it?'

'That's it!' said Kit. 'Oh, I suppose there are also blood-sucking leeches, giant fanged mosquitoes and one particularly large fruit bat called Pipsqueak who seems to have a complex set of anger issues.'

Hamish blinked. He wanted to make sure Kit had actually finished this time.

'And the bull sharks,' Kit said, looking a bit sheepish now. 'And the giant centipede,' he added, opening the doors of the hotel.

Hamish drummed his fingers on his arm as he followed.

'And the tiny little green assassin bug,' Kit said quietly.

Alice began to pull the doors shut behind them.

'But that's it!' said Kit. 'Now go to bed! Your rooms are ready! WE LEAVE AT FIRST LIGHT!'

Hamish and Alice watched him walk off.

'Oh, and guys?' he said, turning around. 'ABP!'

THE DREAM

Thunder.

Thunder so thick and throaty and so loud it seems to grip his ribs.

Hamish blinks in the rain, stopped still in the darkness.

Above him – one by one – the stars in the sky disappear, blown out like candles.

Hamish is small, vulnerable, totally alone – no match for the infinite power of nature.

But this isn't just nature. This is something else. Something unnatural. Something controlling nature.

The wind that moves like a freight train.

The sheets of rain, dense and painful.

It is whatever had dragged Hamish from the coast and now keeps him stuck still in the air.

Now the clouds that had been turning and swirling and forming become something else entirely.

Just a blur right now. But unifying into something.

Hamish squints to make it out, this image like a face pressed against frosted glass.

Oh, he knows that face all too well. *Scarmarsh.*

11

DAYS UNTIL ARRIVAL: 3

It was *hot* in the jungle.

Everyone's socks were already wet and squishy and it was still only early in the morning.

Hamish yawned sleepily and held on to his jungle helmet as Smasha bounced the Monster Patrol All-Terrain Vehicle through the rainforest.

Fat wet vines kept smacking Hamish in the face, though, which was a wonderful way to stay awake.

He had also immediately been hit by the smells of the forest. The flowers, the wood, the strange and mysterious perfume of the plants. It had rained overnight and the soil smelled rich and vibrant. In fact, the whole place was full of life. Hamish felt silly thinking it, but the mix of smells and dark greens really reminded him of his grandad's old greenhouse.

Alice was wide-eyed and alert as she sat up front, helping

Kit find his way. The vehicle they were in looked like a cross between a jeep and a hotel laundry van. It even had a cage hidden in the back just in case the Monster Patrol needed to secretly transport a monster somewhere, while pretending they were just taking underpants and T-shirts to be washed.

'Monster Patrol is so cool!' said Alice, delighted. 'The ship! The jeep! We've just got an old ice-cream van in the PDF!'

Hamish rolled his eyes. It was a very cool ice-cream van, thank you very much. Although he had to admit, this was also a very cool jeep.

Kit had been up most of the night searching Lydia's travel diary for clues, but the map in the photo was still the strongest one. He couldn't believe that all this time they'd been looking in a completely different part of the rainforest.

'Her boot was found here,' said Kit, pointing on a real map at an area of thick trees. 'But from the one in the photo it seems she was heading in this direction.'

'Hmm,' said Alice. 'Literally this whole map is just trees.'

Kit looked awkward.

'Yeah, it's like fourteen ba-jillion square miles of forest.'

Alice and Hamish glanced at each other. Even if they split up, that could take about thirteen hundred years to search.

'First things first,' said Alice, over the buzz of the engine, and trying to take this sensibly. 'Kit, show us where the boot was found.'

'No point,' replied Kit, as Smasha swerved to avoid a fallen tree and burst through some bracken. 'There's nothing to see there any more. It's overgrown. And very dangerous. The last time we were there we detected an increase in monster activity. Probably because we kept turning up and looking at where the boot had been found. Maybe they decided we'd make a nice lunch.'

'Or maybe they were protecting something,' said Hamish,

adjusting his backpack and feeling rather sweaty.

'You said something might have grabbed my grandma,' said Alice. 'Do you think it was the **BÜÜÜÜG**?'

Alice hoped not. **BÜÜÜÜGS** were deadly. And although she knew the reality of the situation, and what fate Lydia might have faced, words like 'deadly' were not words she wanted to think about.

'Maybe,' said Kit. 'But **BÜÜÜÜGS** are more *chasers* than *grabbers*. Whatever it was must have been fast, for her boot to have been pulled off.'

Hamish started to become very concerned about fast-moving monsters. Or fast-moving anythings. Jaguars. Cheetahs. Tiny little green assassin bugs, whatever they were.

'Look,' said Kit. 'There's a reason that hotel is the Monster Patrol HQ. This area is a hotbed of monsters. But trust me: we'd be safest if we avoid the boot area altogether.'

Alice turned to Hamish.

'What do you think?' she said.

'You know what I think,' he smiled.

'We're not here to be safe,' she said, turning back to Kit. 'We're here to find my gran.'

Kit looked at Smasha and shrugged.

Smasha shrugged back, then turned a VERY hard left indeed.

'OW OW OW OW!' yelled Hamish, as Smasha smashed through trees and ferns and rode over hillocks and through bright, rushing streams.

SWASH!
THWACK!
OW!

This was like the worst, most painful fairground ride ever. There were seat belts to hold him in place, but Monster Patrol didn't seem to design their vehicles for comfort. Everything was very boxy and angular and metal.

THWACK!

Hamish didn't understand how he seemed to be the only one being hit by all this stuff. Had he bad-mouthed trees in the past? Were they taking their revenge? Maybe a Venus Spytrap had written a letter to the Plants Complaints Department. Another branch thwacked him in the cakehole, as Alice expertly ducked and weaved around, clinging to the handrail above her, totally focused.

'Y-Y-Y-YOU KNOW WH-WHEN YOU M-M-MENTIONED FAST M-M-MONSTERS?' shouted Hamish, as he bounced around. 'WHAT TYPE?'

'HANG ON A SECOND!' replied Kit.

KA-SPLASH!

The vehicle splashed into the river and bobbed around for a second.

Somehow, Hamish was the only one who got wet.

But was this bad? Were they going to sink?

Smasha pulled a lever and the vehicle's wheels retracted. A small chimney popped out of the roof and started puff-puff-puffing away. Wow. It now seemed to be a boat! Buster would have loved this. Hamish hoped everything was okay back home. He was sure when he and Alice had left, his dad would have gathered the rest of the **PDF** to their HQ in Garage 5 to help with ground support for **Belasko**. Or his friends were coming up with strategies to deal with whatever the Starkley Monster was going to turn out to be. Or maybe they were sitting in their pants watching telly. Hamish knew this trip was important too, especially to Alice, but he hated feeling like he was letting anyone down by not being there.

But if they could find Lydia, well, hopefully that would be the greatest gift he could give Starkley.

As the strange little gang began to float down the river – and curious Bulldog Bats swooped in the air around them – Hamish noticed disconcerting dark shapes shifting around, deep down in the green gunky murkiness around them. Every now and again something broke the surface of the water and immediately pelted and swooshed away again. What was it?

An eel?

A PIRANHA?

Worse?

'Don't panic,' said Kit, sensing Hamish's mood. 'It might just be a Boto.'

'A what-o?' asked Hamish.

'Amazon River Dolphin. Pretty friendly. But keep your arms in, just in case,' said Kit. 'Our last guest didn't. We call him "Lefty" now.'

Hamish and Alice both very quickly and quietly folded their arms. The water around them seemed to get choppier and more active. Giant water lilies bobbed and wobbled around them.

'Uh-oh,' said Kit, scanning the treeline, and

Smasha made an agitated growling noise. 'We're being watched.'

He wasn't kidding. Once Hamish and Alice's eyes got used to the light, as the sun streamed through the treetops and between the leaves and flashed and flickered, all they could see in the dark forest around them were . . .

Eyes.

Big eyes. Little eyes. Things that seemed to have one eye. Things that seemed to have *three* eyes!

'Don't make eye contact,' said Kit, but that was almost impossible, seeing as all you could make contact with were eyes!

And then – just like that . . .

WHOOOOF.

Every single eye that had been watching them closed and then disappeared. The forest shook with the sound of scarpering critters.

'What were they?' asked Alice.

'A bit of everything,' said Kit. 'Probably the odd Jungle Yeti. Maybe one or two Slurms. I definitely smelled a Welsh Rarebit.'

'Why did they suddenly all go?' asked Hamish, even though he definitely knew he didn't want the answer.

'I have a feeling we'll find out soon,' said Kit, tossing a rope at an old dead tree trunk poking out of the water and bringing the boat to a stop.

And Kit was right.

Because the very second they set foot on solid ground, they heard the sound and they smelled the smell.

12

DAYS UNTIL ARRIVAL: 3

This was NOT the way one of these things was supposed to look.

Everyone knows what these things look like. You do. I do. Your mum's great-aunt's neighbour's poodle's vet's dad does. And so does the poodle.

But this was not white. It did not have kind eyes. It did not look like a cuddler. Or a nuzzler. Or like it would take them on a magical adventure, sprinkling stardust in its wake. This was not something you'd put pictures of on wallpaper, or pyjamas, or pillow cases.

This looked like something from a nightmarish otherworld.

Black clawed hooves. Fierce red eyes. Puffing out black fumes, like an old van on a motorway. It reminded Hamish of the Requines – the awful black horses the Terribles had used to storm Starkley back when they first invaded.

But this was . . .

This was . . .

Wait, was this *really* . . .

'A *UNICORN*?' said Alice.

Hamish didn't like this part of the forest. The temperature was cooler here. The soil was blacker. He took a step back and heard the sickening crunch of cockroaches underfoot.

'Be careful!' said Kit, widening his arms protectively, and suddenly wielding a Mon-Stunna, which crackled and fizzed with electric blue energy.

'I thought unicorns were *friendly*!' said Hamish, confused.

'They just have good marketing,' said Kit, for the first time sounding . . . well . . . nervous. 'People think they're white, with a lovely horn, and that they fly along rainbows and drop glitter everywhere. Not the case. Not. At. All.'

And if this unicorn was anything to go by, Kit was right. It did not look happy. And Kit had been right in the plane, too. That was no horn. That was a devilishly sharp and twisted tusk. The unicorn was dirty, and muscular, with a matted mane and wild eyes. And the black fumes pouring from its nostrils reminded Hamish of something else Kit had said earlier.

'Wait . . . did you say they could breathe fire?'

'Of course,' said Kit. 'Unicorns are often used by other monsters to protect themselves. They're the first line of defence against trespassers.'

'Well, how do we beat a unicorn?' said Alice. 'Mister

monster expert?'

Kit shot her a sharp look. It was a look that said two things: a) don't make fun of me, and b) wait, let me think!

The tusked fiend took another step forward, clearly weighing up the danger these four strange figures posed. It sniffed the air, sensing the Mon-Stunna and hearing its crackle and working out its next move.

'Just don't do anything unexpected,' whispered Kit. 'We don't want to startle it.'

All of this did not sit well with Alice. Why wasn't Kit leaping into action? She was fed up with waiting. All she ever seemed to do was wait for monsters or enemies to make the first move. But now she was on a mission. Her grandma might be out there somewhere, nearby even, feeling lost and abandoned and in need of rescuing. No, Alice had things to do. She couldn't hang about all the time, being scared.

I mean, Alice Shepherd – scared?

Of a unicorn?!

'Follow my lead!' she suddenly yelled. **'Raaaargh!'**

She leapt forward, and started clapping her hands together, trying to scare the unicorn off.

'Alice! What are you doing? Kit said

not to do anything unexpected!' shouted Hamish, unsure whether to take his backpack off in case they needed a quick getaway. 'Stop!'

But Alice had had enough of being told to stop all the time. She wanted to *do* something.

She wanted her head checked, is what she wanted.

Seeing her run, the unicorn reared up on to its hind legs and let out a terrifying roar. The jungle seemed to shake around it. But Alice was not stopping. Wild-eyed, she paced forward, shouting and clapping her hands together. Problem was, this was an excellent tactic if you were trying to shoo pigeons. But no one in the world will tell you a unicorn is the same as a pigeon.

Hamish could sense the creature was getting ready to charge. It scraped one hoof on the ground and tensed up. Alice was within spitting distance of it now . . .

'LA LA LA LA LA LA!' shouted Hamish, dancing around and waving his arms in the air. He needed to distract the unicorn for long enough for Alice to understand that she was in grave danger. He looked at Kit desperately. But Kit was backing away, signalling for Smasha to start up the boat again. His Mon-Stunna just looked tiny and pathetic now, in the face of such power and noise.

And then **WHAFF!**

The unicorn swiped its mighty head and bashed Alice out of the way. She flew to the ground, and the unicorn towered above her.

Well, Hamish found himself consumed by rage.

'CHARGE!' he shouted, and he began to run at the unicorn. Because no one and nothing knocked his best friend to the ground. Whether school bully or mythical unicorn!

The unicorn looked startled, as Hamish leapt at it, clinging to its mane. It tried to shake him away, but now Hamish found himself sitting on top of the creature as it began to buck and rear.

'You're supposed to be LOVELY!' screamed Hamish, as he hung on for dear life. **'You're supposed to smell of STRAWBERRIES!'**

RAAAWR roared the unicorn, trying to fling him off.

'You're supposed to dance on RAINBOWS!' shouted Hamish. **'You're supposed to poop CUPCAKES!'**

The unicorn's red eyes glowed brighter and more ferociously. But now Alice had staggered to her feet and seemed to have come to her senses. She'd had a mad moment, fuelled by nothing more than a need to get this unicorn out of the way so she could find Lydia, but by doing that she'd put Hamish in danger.

She looked down for something to throw at the unicorn. **'You're supposed to PEE GLITTER!'** Hamish yelled, and Alice thought he seemed less scared by the unicorn now and more disappointed.

WHOOOOOOOFFFF!

A great blast of FIRE shot from the unicorn's mouth, burning the branches above them and sending clumps of leaves and sticks tumbling to the ground. Insects caught fire in the air and dropped to the floor a second later.

'Guys!' shouted Kit. 'Abandon mission!'

'Where are you going?' Alice yelled at him. 'Come on, Monster Patrol!'

And, as if in response, the unicorn's eyes flashed a deeper blood red, and it REARED into the air, turned on its clawed hooves and THUNDERED away into the jungle, thrashing through bushes, snapping branches clean in two, left, right and centre.

Alice stood staring, powerless.

The unicorn had gone in a split second.

And it had taken poor Hamish with it.

DAYS UNTIL ARRIVAL: 3

Hamish's bottom was getting very sore now.

I mean, it was *really* sore.

Not just from all the bucking and rearing the unicorn was doing, but from the constant powering through the undergrowth and overgrowth and everything-in-between-growth.

It was like getting whacked by a goblin with a badminton racket a thousand times a minute.

OW OW OW OW OW OW OW!

Hamish had no idea what he was going to do. He'd just instinctively jumped for the unicorn when it was threatening Alice. And that, he now realised, was a very silly idea. And *very* bad for his bottom.

THWACK! OW!

Not great for his top either! Another branch slapped him in the face as the unicorn ran and reared past a low-hanging banana tree. Clumps of bananas thudded to the ground with a WHOMP as groups of howler monkeys watched and applauded in delight.

Hamish had no plan other than to just hang on. Sometimes that's the only plan anyone ever has. And even though he really wanted to get off this unicorn, he knew that getting off this unicorn would be the worst thing possible. If he got off the unicorn, he'd be *lost in the jungle*. Alone! At least he knew exactly where he was – he was on a unicorn! And although this terrifying fire-breathing unicorn wasn't the *best* company, sometimes you've just got to take what you can get, don't you? And sometimes that *will* mean hanging out with an awful mythical beast.

THWACK! OW!

Was the unicorn doing this on PURPOSE? It seemed very angry about having Hamish on its back. Furious, even. As well as charging through bushes, it would occasionally spin around like a Waltzer, clearly trying to get rid of the ten-year-old boy who was clinging on to its back for dear life. That was another reason Hamish didn't want to get off the creature: what it might do to him when he did!

No, he had to cling on no matter what. No matter where this unicorn might be going.

Wait . . . What if this unicorn was taking him somewhere specific? Like, to *other* fearsome unicorns? Or to the gruesome **BÜÜÜÜG**? Was this what had happened to poor Lydia?

THWACK! OW!

Hamish was getting really annoyed at the trees now, and you know someone's annoyed when they can get annoyed at *trees*. As he shielded his eyes from more branch attacks while keeping a very firm fist wrapped around the unicorn's tusk, Hamish noticed the ground beneath them had become worn. Almost like a path. This wasn't a random journey into the jungle any more. This was a known one. A well-travelled one.

And then Hamish's stomach leapt.

Up ahead, maybe ten seconds away at this great speed, was a clearing.

And just beyond the clearing, Hamish could see a gap between that piece of land and another.

A very *large* gap.

'Stop, unicorn!' shouted Hamish. 'Whoa, boy! Or girl! Or whatever you are!'

But the unicorn wasn't stopping. In fact, it was speeding up. Galloping. Head low, hooves thundering . . .

He could see the gap now. It wasn't just a gap. This was a ravine. It was like the Grand Canyon. The closer he got, the wider it seemed, like zooming out on a camera and seeing the whole picture.

He'd seen films. He'd seen cartoons. He knew that a drop like this probably wasn't good. They couldn't leap that. Nothing could. This unicorn was mad.

Hamish had maybe a second to decide what to do . . . jump? Or stay?

Too late!

Hamish leaned into the unicorn. Pressed his head against its muscular neck. Gripped its tusk tighter. Closed his eyes. Gritted his teeth. Held his breath.

And when they were just centimetres from the edge, and as Hamish knew that the cavernous drop was below him, the unicorn

L
E
A
P
T!

The leap seemed to last forever...

Then...

He rose, and he rose, and he seemed to *fly*!

Fly for just a moment, but it was still a moment, wasn't it?

Travelling far further and far faster and far higher than Hamish had been expecting!

And when they landed with a JOLT and the unicorn stopped still immediately and unexpectedly, Hamish was flung from its back and bounced heavily into the undergrowth, his Monster Patrol backpack breaking his fall.

He stared up at the canopy of trees above him, the sunlight dappling through. His fingers raked the wet soil beneath him.

He had survived!

And then the unicorn's face came clear into view, and Hamish felt its hot and sour breath on his face.

He realised that about *now* would be a cracking time to have a plan.

14

DAYS UNTIL ARRIVAL: 3

'Well, fat lot of good you were,' said Alice to Kit, grumpily, as she pushed vast broken branches out of the way. 'Monster Patrol. Pah!'

They were making slow progress in the heat, moving past Lobster Claw flowers and Monkey Brush vines, following the trail of devastation and trampled ferns and bushes the unicorn had left in its wake.

'I never said I was any good!' said Kit. 'To be honest, I'm more of a monster enthusiast than a monster *expert* or *fighter*. But I'm trying!'

'You're suddenly very trying,' agreed Alice, resting for a second by a rubber tree. 'And now Hamish is lost in the jungle at the mercy of a unicorn while time ticks away in Starkley. You just went for the boat! Why didn't you even try your stunny thing?'

'It's basically just a toy,' said Kit, sadly. His previous

confidence had all but vanished. 'I put it together because sometimes it frightens the smaller monsters.'

Alice slapped her forehead. This was a disaster. And Kit seemed rather less impressive now. One thing was for sure: Monster Patrol was turning out to be no **PDF**.

'Look,' said Kit, scrambling to catch up with Alice as she strode forward again. 'That's why I need to find Lydia. She was the expert. She can teach us all. The world needs Monster Patrol and only she can bring it back properly!'

'So what *can* you do?' said Alice, spying more broken branches and realising the unicorn must have dragged poor Hamish that way.

'Well . . . the odd spell.'

'Oh, great,' said Alice, sighing. 'We're back to "magic", are we?'

Alice was a very practical girl. The type of girl who'd see a magician doing a card trick and immediately work out how they'd done it, how they could do it better, and how much they were probably getting paid to deceive the public.

'I know it sounds weird,' said Kit. 'Lydia was always very scientific, like **Belasko**. Because **Belasko** likes "science" and "gadgets" and "facts". I told you my grandmamma was a little more experimental. She was trying techniques **Belasko** did not approve of.'

'Is that what Hamish's dad meant when he said Monster Patrol had changed?'

'Some would of course call what we tried "magic", but we say it was not exactly magic. Because when "magic" works, you no longer call it magic. When it works, then it is *science*.'

Alice rolled her eyes. If his monster hunting skills were anything to go by, she could only imagine this 'magic' and these 'spells' were the most rubbish spells possible, like spells for moving a spoon very slightly or making a beetle dance.

'And what about him?' she said, nodding at Smasha. 'So you and a silent giant puffer fish just wander around, doing card tricks and waving toys at monsters, do you?'

Kit and Smasha looked at each other, aghast.

'How *RUDE*!' said Smasha, and Alice stopped in her tracks.

Had that Puffox thing really spoken?

'You can speak!' she said.

'Of course I can speak,' said Smasha, who actually sounded quite posh, like he belonged in a country house somewhere fancy, like the Palace of Westmonster.

'Then why *didn't* you speak?'

'Because *you* didn't speak to *me*!' he said, indignant. 'You simply strode on to our plane, gave me one look, and decided I couldn't speak. And I know exactly why!'

'Why?' asked Alice.

'It was because of my *fish head*, wasn't it?'

'Uh, well . . . sort of,' said Alice.

'Typical! You see a monster who *happens* to have a fish head and decide they can't speak. You probably think I have some kind of special fish-head language and only hang out with special fish-head people, do you?'

Alice looked ashamed.

'A bit.'

'Well, just because I *look different to you* doesn't mean we have nothing in common,' said Smasha, stepping carefully to avoid damaging an orchid. 'And Kit has always treated me with respect!'

'I'm sorry.'

'Are you?' said Smasha. 'Because remember: we may not be the world's best monster hunters, but we are the best chance you've got. And monster hunter runs through that boy's veins every bit as much as it runs through yours!'

Alice stared at her feet.

'I've been helping him with his words,' said Kit quietly.

'Puffoxes are highly intelligent, but they're also very sensitive. He's been in a real mood with you since you got onboard.'

'So rude,' Smasha muttered, behind them. 'And you didn't even say thank you for your lunchboxes. Who do you think was up all night cracking a cactus in two so you'd have a lovely lunch?'

'I'm very sorry,' said Alice, flicking a bright blue bug from her shoulder. 'Please can we start again?'

She stared at them very seriously.

'Look, we all want to find Lydia. You want to find your leader. I want to find my grandma. And Hamish wants to find a saviour for Starkley. But right now we're lost in the jungle, and Hamish has been captured by a unicorn. It might be scaring him. It might be eating him! It might be using its sharp tusks, devilish claws and its fire-breathing FURY to torture him! So we had better hurry, because we need Hamish Ellerby – he's not just my best friend, he's one of the bravest people I know – and right now Hamish Ellerby is in *deep, deep trouble!*'

15

DAYS UNTIL ARRIVAL:
STILL 3, YES

Hamish had never been licked so much in his life.

As it turned out, unicorns weren't so bad when you got to know them!

There was the smell, of course. It smelled like a match catching fire. And you had to be really careful around that sharp tusk. And if it nuzzled into your chest, it'd leave black marks all over your top, like smudged ink, or soot. But apart from that there was mainly the licking and sniffing.

Sniff. Sniff. SNIFF.

Since it had managed to get rid of the weird human who just wouldn't get off its back, the unicorn could not help but be curious. His huge sandpapery tongue had given Hamish's hair quite the cowlick. But now it wasn't Hamish he was interested in. It was those strange light green squares in his hand.

They looked clean. Pure. This unicorn was used to dirty things, covered in mud, or dirt, or moss. These seemed *pristine*.

It leaned forward, and with one quick lick from a tongue the size of a cushion, gobbled a cactus sugar cube down.

CHOMP.

SNAFFLE.

SWALLOW.

For a second, nothing happened. The unicorn just seemed startled. Its eyes weren't red now; they were white, bright and interested. There were no fumes at all.

Giving it a sugar lump had been all Hamish could think to do. Now he wondered, peeling his banana and taking a bite . . . had he *tamed the unicorn*!?

He reached up, thinking he might like to pet the creature. And though the unicorn was suspicious, it let Hamish touch its mane, and the short fringe at the base of its tusk.

'Good uni,' said Hamish, calmly, as great big palm leaves swooshed and swayed around him. 'Now . . . do you think I could ride you back to the others?'

The unicorn stared at him blankly.

'Like, maybe I could just climb back on, and you could

magically jump over that gap again?' he said, smiling, as if that might help. 'Because we need to hopefully find this woman who disappeared a long time ago so that we can reunite her with her granddaughter and then get her back to my town so that we can save it from a sea monster.'

Hamish tried the 'angel face' he usually made when meeting other children's parents, and gave the unicorn a charming smile. Maybe it would understand that?

The unicorn licked his face again, and Hamish giggled and gave its head another tickle.

But as he did, he noticed something, and his hand froze still.

There was something just under the unicorn's fringe.

Curious, he brushed the hair to one side, and revealed a very distinctive mark.

Hamish's heart nearly stopped still.

He had seen a mark just like this before.

It was the same size and almost the exact same shape as one he was all too familiar with.

'Scarmarsh,' muttered Hamish.

He took a step back, feeling sick at the memory of the evil genius's scar.

What did that mean? Was it coincidence? Did Axel

Scarmarsh own this unicorn?

No . . . no, it was impossible.

Hamish stared again at the mark. He reached out, touched it, feeling sick as he did so.

A thousand ideas spun through Hamish's head at once. Was Scarmarsh everywhere? In his dreams, in this jungle? Did his powers know no bounds? If Scarmarsh controlled the unicorn, what else might he control? Armies of gorgons, or griffins, or cyclopses, or yetis, or dragons? He could raise serpents, and giant moths – maybe Godzilla itself!

He rubbed at the mark on the unicorn's head, willing it to disappear.

And with relief, he saw that it was coming off. . .

It was just dirt.

Dirt picked up on their mad gallop through the bushes.

He felt like laughing and crying all at once.

Would he ever be rid of his fear of this man? If he was even seeing his presence in places he couldn't possibly be?

But as well as relief, Hamish felt paranoid. Like he was being watched. He felt like he might never be rid of Scarmarsh, and not just because he was related to him. And now here he was, stuck in a jungle, a million miles from home, confused and separated from his friends.

He stepped back again, his tummy churning and the rainforest seeming to twist and whirl around him.

Which way had they come? Where was the ravine? How could he make it back over? Where would he sleep tonight? How would he protect himself? What would he eat? What would happen when night came? Could he trust the unicorn?

And as he stumbled further and further back, and the jungle spun faster around him, he tripped on something heavy, hidden in the long grass.

Hamish fell back on to the roots of a Babassu tree, hitting his head, hard.

A DIFFERENT DREAM

'What is this?' Hamish asks himself.

No longer is he at the cliffs, nor above the swirling waters of the sea.

He blinks in total silence.

No wind, no rain. No streak of bright silver shooting from blackened clouds, no brooding booms of thunder to shake him like a doll.

No, now Hamish sits in a room, lit by a single candle in the centre of a very long table.

He can feel the coldness of the walls without touching them. He feels their height instinctively, but he can see no doors. He spins around, noticing just a pinprick of light somewhere high above.

And as he looks back down . . . a figure sits at the other end of the table.

His stomach lurches.

He wants to speak, he wants to know where he is, but the words stick in his throat. He feels small, but the anger in his stomach has grown.

When these dreams started, they had just been silly dreams, embarrassing, horrible, but just normal dreams. Then they changed and he had started to feel the sea spray on his face, the wind in his hair.

And now he feels it all. The hardness of his chair. The splinter digging into the back of his leg. He can taste the tang of moss from the walls. He can feel his eyes adjusting as the candle flickers in front of the figure just beyond it.

'What do you want?' Hamish finally manages to say. He'd wanted to say it forcefully, angrily, to show this man he was no pushover, and he didn't appreciate his dreams being invaded this way.

But Hamish doesn't need a reply.

Because Hamish already knows the answer.

16

DAYS UNTIL ARRIVAL: 3

'Tell me more about the boot you found,' said Alice, as Smasha sniffed the ground and led the way.

'Well, it was Lydia's,' said Kit. 'A cherry red army boot. If a unicorn had grabbed her in the same place, it must have given her quite a shake.'

They had been following the trail for some time now, feeling a bit hopeless, but completely unaware that they were actually catching up with a largely unconscious Hamish.

'I suppose you never found the second boot?' asked Alice.

'Look!' said Smasha. 'Banana fruit! Hither and thither! I should therefore assume they most definitely came this way.'

Alice felt sorry for Smasha. It must be very tiring talking that way the whole time.

The forest was getting darker the deeper they travelled.

'How long have you known Hamish?' asked Kit.

'Actually not that long,' said Alice. 'But we've had enough adventures to make it seem a lifetime. Why?'

'My grandmamma was a great believer in dreams and their power. She believed you could get important messages through them.'

'What's that got to do with me and Hamish?' asked Alice. 'And, if it's true, then how come all my dreams are about random stuff, like swimming in a pool full of snooker balls that turn out to be my teacher?'

'Okay, not all dreams mean things,' said Kit. 'But my grandmamma would tell me about some of hers. And she told me one about a town that was under attack from a great unknown. The town was cut off from help from the outside. She described it so perfectly. And when I got to Starkley, well . . . it really reminded me of it.'

Alice grew uncomfortable.

'How did the dream end?' she said.

'All she said was that she saw a boy, a chosen one, standing on a cliff top. His clothes blowing wildly in the wind. A kid you'd never suspect might be the answer. And with the help of his friends, only *he* could vanquish the monster when called.'

'Hamish . . .' whispered Alice.

'Oh dear!' shouted Smasha, up ahead. 'We have company!'

Alice immediately struck a karate pose. Kit pulled out his Mon-Stunna and crackled it to life. From above them came a terrifying . . .

HOOOOOOWWWWLLL!

The noise grew and grew until it seemed to be everywhere, coming from every angle possible.

'Howler monkeys!' yelled Kit.

'Monkeys?' said Alice. 'Oh, I love monkeys!'

Suddenly, to her left, a monkey dropped from a tree. Two more landed beside it.

They stood on their hind legs.

They were much taller than she'd imagined, with long and scrawny arms. They began to walk towards her, menacingly.

These monkeys did not look friendly, with pinched faces, scarred legs and mean eyes.

More monkeys scooted down trees and shrieked at them, and, in the trees above, others yelled and shook the branches, sending bits of the trees tumbling down. Two of the ones on the ground pushed Smasha back into the trees.

'Get off!' he shouted. 'Stop monsterhandling me!'

Kit and Alice stood back to back, as more muscular primates circled them aggressively.

'What do we do?' said Alice. 'I've never fought a monkey!'

'Get back!' yelled Kit, waving his pretend weapon in front of him to no effect whatsoever.

A howler lunged at Alice, its little fingers prodding her, hard. It was testing the water, seeing what she'd do and if she could defend herself. They'd probably never seen many humans before. They must have wondered what these strange bald monkeys were.

Kit stepped forward. He knew this was his chance to redeem himself in Alice's eyes. But he seemed uncertain again.

'Can't you do a spell?' said Alice, desperately, as the atmosphere turned more dangerous. 'You said you can do spells!'

'I can, but not very well!' said Kit.

'Oh, just try it!'

But Kit had another plan.

'SMASHA!' he shouted. **'MONSTER UP!'**

Immediately, Smasha thundered out of the undergrowth – he'd torn off his boiler suit to reveal his full Puffox body and he seemed bigger and badder than he had before. There was no posh voice now – just the full and throaty ROAR of a *proper monster*!

The monkeys that had been clambering over him began to screech and panic. A few others fled, leaping up trees and swinging away. But the bigger ones raised their arms and made their war cries and stepped forward, challenging this weird furfish to make his stand.

Which is when the Puffox began to shake.

And tremble.

And positively vibrate.

And grow.

Not just his hands, and arms, and body . . .

But his *whole head*!

BA-POFF!

Smasha's puffer fish head rapidly inflated to THREE TIMES its normal size!

Kit and Alice dove for cover as the monkeys began to squeal. Smasha waved his arms around and bared his four teeth and stomped his feet like a New Zealand rugby player doing a haka!

Well, this was pretty terrifying for most of the monkeys. (*You're* quite monkey-like – imagine how *you'd* feel if a big weirdo with a fish face suddenly inflated its head at you!)

And, as Smasha started to fire off small poison darts that whizzed through the air, the monkeys knew that this was a monster that meant business.

'YES, Smasha!' shouted Alice, punching the air. **'Be the monster you were meant to be! Live your best monster life!'**

Smasha jumped up and down, firing darts high into the air which tore through leaves and rained down around the monkeys. The animals fled, howling and screeching and bounding from tree to tree, until the noise of their calls faded into the distance.

Kit watched them go, his face a genuine picture of relief.

'Howler monkeys don't usually attack,' he said, confused. 'They just let you pass.'

'Well, I'll take it personally then,' said Alice.

'No,' said Kit. 'It means we're heading in the right direction. Those monkeys were meant to stop us. Maybe they were placed here by the Superiors many years ago to warn people off. It shows that we're not just on the way to find Hamish. We're on the way to find *Lydia*.'

He got his map out and studied their position. His face fell.

'But there may well be a pretty big problem first.'

Hamish came round feeling dizzy and confused by his latest dream, as well as being sore all over.

He had a sore head from where he'd knocked himself out on the Babassu tree.

He had a sore bottom from riding a unicorn at a thousand miles an hour.

He had a sore face from being constantly thwacked by every branch he seemed to pass.

And he had a sore tummy from eating one very green banana.

So, generally, he was sore. And he was also a bit grumpy now.

'What did I trip on?' he said, still flat on his back, as the unicorn nudged his face to make sure he was okay. 'I will have my REVENGE!'

Oh, he would pick up that stone and throw it as far as he could.

Or, if it was a log, he'd give it a good kick.

Or, if it was a frog or something, he'd say something that might really hurt its feelings.

He stood up and strode over to the patch of long grass

that had been his downfall.

'There's something in there,' he said, tapping at it with his foot. He still had to be careful. This was the jungle after all.

He peered closer.

Whatever it was, it was **WET**.

It had dark red, **LEATHERY** skin.

It had a dozen or so **HOLES** along its belly, and these holes looked almost like **AWFUL SUCKERS**.

It had wrapped its own long, loose **TENTACLES** across its saggy belly, and let them **TRAIL** either side of it, as if resting.

Its lazy **TONGUE** lolloped out, spilling from its neck, and its whole body **ARCHED** upwards, as if stretching.

And it was perfectly **STILL**, which made Hamish think it might be about to **STRIKE**!

He thought about tiptoeing away and forgetting the whole revenge thing.

And then he blinked once or twice and stared at it properly.

'That's not an animal.'

He picked the item up between two fingers. It was heavy and weather-beaten. It had holes in the bottom, perhaps from where a mouse or rat had made its home. Yeeeuch. Hamish was about to toss it to one side, when two thoughts struck him.

'How did this get here?' he said. 'And who brought it?'

As he looked at it, Hamish suddenly realised this could be the most important old cherry red army boot in the world.

17

DAYS UNTIL ARRIVAL: 3

Kit had spotted the huge drop on the map immediately and reasoned that, somewhere, there had to be a bridge across.

They had walked all the way to the edge, but it was way too steep to climb down, and far too wide to jump.

'Smasha,' said Kit. 'Get back to the hotel. Bring the Astral Plane, okay? If all else fails, you can fly us across.'

'But that'll take ages!' said Alice. 'Poor Hamish is out there somewhere. And so's Grandma Lydia, probably. And time's running out for Starkley!'

'I shall be as quick as possible, ma'am,' said Smasha, a little sarcastically Alice thought, and then darted off into the undergrowth. Sadly, his head was still inflated, and he kept piercing leaves on his spikes. He would be very handy to have in the garden in the autumn, thought Alice. You could just roll him around and pick up all the leaves.

Now it was just her and Kit, Alice felt a bit uncomfortable.

She had forgiven him now, because she'd realised that really her anger was just a need to blame someone for what had happened, and Kit's plan with the monkeys had worked in the end . . . But she just felt safer around Hamish. And now she'd managed to lose him to a unicorn, which was not a sentence she'd ever expected to think.

Kit, however, seemed unconcerned. He was kneeling on the ground, studying something.

'The soil is dry on this side,' he said. 'But over on that side, it seems damper. Look at the plants.'

In the distance, above the trees, Alice could make out some kind of tall hill, covered in rich vines and trees. It looked like a tropical playground.

Kit suddenly started to sniff the ground, which – in Alice's honest opinion – was not a good look.

'Mapinguari,' he said.

'Bless you,' said Alice.

'No. Mapinguari is a sort of giant sloth,' said Kit. 'Seven feet tall. They stink. They move silently through the jungle, but they're heavy, hence the footprints.'

Alice looked where Kit was now pointing. She couldn't see any footprints. Maybe he was quite useful after all. Unless there were no footprints, and he was just mad. After all, he said he could do spells but so far had absolutely failed to do even one.

'But why would a Mapinguari be at the edge of a drop like this?' Kit said to himself.

'Because it's looking for something?' suggested Alice. 'For a way across?'

Kit clicked his fingers as if to say 'Yes!'

'It went that way,' said Kit, and they set off, trampling through the bushes, making sure not to fall off the edge of the cliff.

Uni could not stop sniffing that boot.

To be frank, Hamish had started to think it was a bit weird.

But the unicorn was obviously excited. It shoved its nose straight inside the boot and waggled it around, snorting and rearing all the while. It looked like it had found its first toy.

'Okay,' said Hamish. 'Maybe we could head back now?'

Hamish knew it was silly just to talk English to a mythical creature in a foreign land, but they didn't teach Unicorn Studies at Winterbourne School. Perhaps he'd suggest it to Frau Fussbundler when he got home.

If he got home.

Hamish decided if he started to walk back the way they came, maybe Uni would get the message.

But every time he stepped away, Uni clamped on to his jumper and pulled him back.

'Friends,' said Hamish, pointing back towards the trees. 'My friends!'

Uni was having none of it. Instead he kept trying to lead Hamish further into the trees, like a dog who wanted to play.

Hamish didn't know what to do. He didn't want to go with the unicorn and keep heading away from Alice and Kit. But he also didn't want to be alone and lost. If all else failed, he could try and clamber on its back again and see where he ended up. At least that gave him a chance of finding help.

So, begrudgingly, Hamish followed the unicorn deeper into the jungle.

'Aha!' said Kit. 'Look!'

In front of them was exactly what Alice did not want to see.

A rope bridge.

A thin, wobbly rope bridge.

Frayed.

Creaking in the wind.

Swaying a little too much.

A single jungle rat darted across it, with nimble and quick little feet that Alice felt quite jealous of. The rat stopped near the centre of the bridge to chew on some rope, then dashed away again.

'Well, it's a real pity there's absolutely no way we can use this bridge,' said Alice. 'We'll have to find another way.'

'Ha!' said Kit, deciding the founder member of the **PDF** must be joking. 'Come on!'

He stepped one foot on to the bridge and looked back at her. The whole thing drooped slightly and the wooden stakes it was attached to shifted in the dirt.

'People have been using this bridge for years, I'll bet,' said Kit, trying to be reassuring, before adding quietly: 'Just don't look down because you might spot some of them.' Alice's eyes widened. She was all for action, but this did not look safe. It did not sound safe. It did not feel safe. Putting all this evidence together, she decided this probably meant it wasn't safe.

But Kit took another step, and the bridge held.

'It's okay,' he said, offering her his hand. 'This is what Monster Patrolling is all about!'

She took it, and stepped on.

'How come you were so worried about your spell back there with the monkeys?' said Alice. 'I mean, it's okay if you can't do spells at all and you were just saying it to sound impressive.'

The bridge lowered slightly again.

'I can do spells,' said Kit. 'Sometimes I just lack confidence. I get worried it won't work or I'll look stupid or not strong.'

'Everyone worries about that sometimes,' said Alice, who'd only stepped on to this awful bridge because she was worried she wouldn't look strong.

The creak of the wooden stakes got louder.

'Maybe we should hurry a bit?' said Alice, and she and Kit now held both sides of this swaying, wobbly bridge. There was only one long rope from one side to the other for them to stand on. It was like tightrope walking.

They were halfway there now.

'Keep going,' said Kit. 'Just keep looking forward.'

But something odd was happening up ahead. A mild commotion.

The jungle rat had seemed very keen to get away from

them before. But now Alice could see it again. It was panicking, squealing, and pounding at them. It jumped back on the rope bridge and shot past them, scrabbling around them and not even stopping to gnaw at the bridge.

Kit and Alice exchanged a glance. Something must have spooked it. Every instinct they had was telling them to turn around, but . . .

BOMF!

The bridge dropped another few centimetres.

'Those stakes aren't going to hold!' said Kit, stealing a glance at the trembling and straining pieces of wood behind them.

'RUN!' said Alice, and the two kids immediately sprinted for the other side . . .

And as they did, the stakes were pulled from the soil by the weight of them, and the bridge began to fall behind them with a **CRASH** as they **LEAPT** to the other side and rolled on to the ground in the nick of time.

And then . . .

. . . there was a noise.

18

DAYS UNTIL ARRIVAL: 3

There were three of them this time.

POWERFUL.

MUSCULAR.

EMOTIONLESS.

Oh, it was hard to know what these brooding, thunder-like unicorns were thinking, but it was easy to guess.

They were thinking you *shouldn't* be here.

They were thinking you *need* to leave.

They were thinking you *will* regret this.

The three unicorns stalked around Kit and Alice, towering over the kids and snorting diesel-black fumes into their faces.

'Uh, maybe we shouldn't have sent Smasha away,' said Alice, trying to put on her Angel Face to show how totally unthreatening she was to unicorns. Sadly, Alice's Angel Face was generally about as effective as a cardboard snorkel.

'This is bad,' said Kit. 'Three unicorns. A triumvirate.

According to legend, unicorns that travel in threes are sent into battle by their leader. The solitary ones are pages, messengers, sentries. But a trio of unicorns . . . that spells trouble.'

'What are they going to do to us?' said Alice, hoping the answer might be 'tickle us' or 'treat us to a lovely cup of soup'.

'I think it's better I don't say,' said Kit, reaching for his Mon-Stunna and switching it on.

But nothing happened. It had a large crack in its side, obviously from their hard landing.

'Well, your toy's knackered,' said Alice, through gritted teeth. 'I'm carrying one green banana and some tea bags.'

Kit ignored her and continued to stare at the Mon-Stunna.

Alice lost patience again. This was ridiculous! How could you call yourself the leader of something like Monster Patrol if all you could do was walk on bridges and spot footprints in the soil and break your toy gun?

'Do you, Kit Alexander Lopez – *as the only human member of Monster Patrol on Earth* – have *anything else* that might *actually help with monsters* at all?' Alice said.

Kit looked at her, weighing something up, trying to decide whether now was the right moment.

And he took off his bag.

And he brought something out.

A chain. Some kind of medallion.

No, not a medallion.

Alice had seen one of these in the *Wunderkammer* on board the ship.

It was a claw.

Kit put the chain and claw around his neck and looked nervously at Alice.

He was going to try something.

Sensing his hesitation, Alice decided to change tack, realising that now was not the time to be annoyed. Now was the time to be encouraging.

'You can do it,' she said. 'Don't worry!'

Kit took a deep breath and began to murmur.

He raised his arms to his waist.

And a moment or three later, small flashes and flares began to crackle and burst in the air around him. Like fireworks seen from twenty miles away.

Alice stepped back, amazed.

Was this … *magic*?!

Kit smiled, and grew in confidence, and raised his arms high into the air.

Alice stepped back. Whatever Kit was doing was angering and confusing the unicorns. And they were getting ready to strike. She was frightened. But something was happening and it was indeed . . . *magical*. She took cover behind a tree, as Kit suddenly stopped his murmurs and shouted . . .

'AND IT SHALL BE SO NOW!'

POW!

Alice slammed her hands to her mouth in awe.

Kit was no longer Kit. His hands were growing into paws. His fingers had become claws. His ears were pointy and sharp and above his head, and his nose was now wet and black.

And the teeth!

Kit was furry. Kit was *fury*.

Kit was . . .

'A werewolf?' whispered Alice.

Kit was a monster himself.

But wait, thought, Alice – *only temporarily*! Kit's gran had

taught him that spell. And it
would make sense to fight monsters with monsters!

But Kit hadn't finished.

He was still growing . . . his back arching upwards, the
bones in his body crackling as they became bigger and
more powerful.

The unicorns were more aggressive now and seemed

ready to blow fire and fury of their own. They surrounded Kit, but with one powerful SWIPE, he knocked one into the ravine.

It fell and fell, until it had the sense to flap out two wings and speed off into the distance.

The other unicorns tried their best, but were no match for a giant werewolf.

They fled, **SCREECHING** so loudly they could be heard for miles.

They could be heard, in fact, by Hamish.

🐾

'Guys!' said Hamish, arriving through the bushes on Uni. 'I found you! Well, we found you.'

He gave Uni's mane a little stroke as Alice punched the air at seeing her friend again.

'Wait,' she said. 'You've befriended that unicorn?!'

'He's a bit licky, but you get used to that,' said Hamish. 'Hey, where's Smasha? Where's Kit?'

Why was Alice all alone in the jungle?

'Smasha's gone to get the plane,' she said. 'And Kit's, uh, a bit shy.'

'Huh?'

'I'M GETTING CHANGED!' came a voice from

the jungle.

Basically, as I'm sure you know, when you turn into a werewolf it tends to rip all your clothes off. So it was lucky Kit always carried a spare uniform in his bag.

'Things have been a little traumatic since you galloped off on your new pal,' said Alice.

'Well, follow me,' said Hamish. 'Because I think we've made *quite* the discovery . . .'

19

DAYS UNTIL ARRIVAL: 3 (IT WAS A LONG DAY, OKAY?)

'Uni brought me here,' said Hamish, leading the gang through a thicket towards higher ground. 'A cave! I found a boot, and he sniffed it, and I guess he recognised the scent? What if it's . . . Lydia's?'

'Büüüüg droppings,' said Kit, pointing at a teetering pile of dirt outside the entrance.

Kit had asked Alice not to mention the whole werewolf thing to Hamish just yet. People reacted strangely to magic, when it worked. Everybody seemed to love the idea of it, but when they realised it was real, well, they would look at him differently. As if he was freakish somehow. It had happened a lot in his life. That's why he preferred hanging around with Smasha. That's why he didn't really have many other friends. But the science of magic, he'd told Alice, was about belief. If you don't believe in magic, then magic won't exist. A spell won't work unless you believe it will, and the more belief there is, the more powerful the spell.

'But science isn't about just *believing* something is true,' said Alice.

'It is, if *belief* is a real thing,' Kit had said. 'If it is a real feeling – as real as feeling hungry or happy and it is powerful and present and undeniable – it becomes part of the formula!'

If Alice hadn't seen it happen with her own eyes, she'd have thought it sounded like hokum. She wished she could tell Hamish. As I'm sure you can imagine, usually the second you find out someone can become a werewolf, you're pretty desperate to shout 'they can become a WEREWOLF!', aren't you?

Kit traced his finger down the walls of the entrance. There was a strange, gooey, neon green liquid all around it, as if the mouth of the cave had applied some really disgusting lipstick.

'BÜÜÜÜG snot,' said Kit, gravely.

'Then this must be its lair!' said Alice. 'Unless BÜÜÜÜGS use caves as hankies or something.'

She looked around to make sure no more unicorns were anywhere to be seen. Uni bridled, nervously. Hamish

reached into Alice's bag and tossed Uni
one of her cactus sugar lumps.

'Only one thing for it, Alice,' Hamish said,
puffing out his chest and trying to be brave. 'We go in.'

The hole was small so Hamish had to de-puff his chest
almost immediately. Goodness knows how a mighty
Büüüüg could fit through that. Hamish wondered if that
meant there was another opening elsewhere. This might
just be a secret back door, used for quick escapes or sneaky
entrances.

The ground at the mouth of the cave was covered in
small loose rocks and cave chippings that crunched as they
stepped in. The kids watched their shadows blend in with
the darkness inside, as if they were melting into the gloom.
They guided themselves by placing their hands on the wet
walls. Above them, sharp stalactites stretched towards the
ground.

'Anything could be in here,' said Kit. 'Bats. Spiders.
Snakes.'

Uni snorted, obviously not a fan of bats, or spiders, or
snakes.

'Can't be worse than a BÜÜÜÜG,' whispered Alice,
conscious that she didn't want to start an echo if she couldn't

be sure what might hear it. 'They have bug eyes, and wings, and claws, and teeth, and all sorts of other horrible things.'

'Alice,' whispered Hamish, feeling less brave and a bit queasier now. 'Maybe we could focus on the positives of the situation?'

Alice nodded and tried to think of some.

She couldn't.

Further in they went. Hamish was actually quite glad that Uni was here. This was his world, after all . . .

Kit fished out a torch from his bag and shone it around. There were pools of stagnant water around them. A beetle the size of a cat scuttled away to find darker corners.

'Look,' said Alice, as they carefully squeezed through a narrow gap in the cave walls. The rocks were jagged and uneven and the kids had to be careful not to bump their heads.

Up ahead, some way off, they could make out a tiny pinprick of light. Hamish's heart was beating loudly in his ears. It's not normal to be somewhere so dark. Somewhere the sun or the moon can't reach, and where time suddenly seems to have no meaning.

As they got through the gap, the smell of wet rock and old water hung heavy in the air. The pinprick of light was easier to see now, and with every careful, crunchy step they took it grew bigger. It was impossible to see what that light was. There were no details. It just looked like a sheet of white light, until finally it was right in front of them.

'Whoa,' said Kit, putting his hand out carefully. This was obviously the entrance to something. But it was covered and shielded by some kind of thick silvery fabric. It shimmered in the light that came from directly behind it. It was dense, though it flapped very lightly from a sudden small breeze.

'This is a web,' said Kit. 'A Büüüüg web.'

'So we're in the right place,' said Alice, pushing her hand into the web to try and brush it away. 'Gosh, this stuff is tough.'

Hamish had a go next. He tried to poke a hole in the web with his finger, but it was

impossible. It just sprang
back, like an impenetrable
skin on some old custard.

'Büüüüg webs are incredibly
tough,' said Kit. 'This is the
result of years of work.'

'There has to be a way,' said Alice,
picking up a rock and hurling it at the
web, then watching it bounce straight
back and roll to her feet.

Hamish tried to give it a shoulder-barge, but
this stuff was just not giving.

'Wait,' said Alice. 'Listen!'

They could hear noise, now.

There was the gentle noise of running water.

But underneath it, there was a low, rumbling,
grumble.

A noise that rose and fell. It was rhythmic. It
was unsettling, strange, but somehow familiar.

'Wait,' said Alice. 'Is that . . . *snoring*?'

Alice knew this sound all too well. Her mum

and dad were major
snorers and sometimes
the pictures on her bedroom
wall would rattle from the sound of her
dad's naps.

'What if it's the BÜÜÜÜG?'
said Hamish.

'Or what,' said Alice, 'if it's Lydia?'

'We need to take a closer look without waking
whatever that is,' said Kit. 'But there's no way
through. It's too tough to cut without special
equipment.'

Which is when Hamish had an idea.

'Hey, Kit,' he said. 'You said unicorn tusks are the
sharpest things known to mankind, right?'

The kids all turned to Uni.

Uni sliced through the BÜÜÜÜG web in
a heartbeat, and Kit chucked him a cactus
sugar cube.

They stepped through the web, parting it

like curtains, and into the brightness
of the unknown.

They were not prepared for what
they saw next.

The cave widened right out. High above
them, a hole in the ceiling let bright sunlight pour
all the way down to the cave floor. Hamish shivered.
The hole reminded him of the dream he'd had when
he'd been knocked out by the tree.

But it was what they saw when they looked down that
was really incredible.

There were coconut trees on the ground, stretching
towards the sun on patches of bright green grass. There were
flowers and strange berries. A stream of noisy fresh water
ran down one side of the cave walls and into a small, clean
rock pool at the bottom. Narrow wooden gutters had
been put up around the walls, transporting water
to different parts of the cave, including a small
kitchen area full of old coconut shells. There
were shelves made from fallen branches, and
a table, and colourful paintings etched into the

walls above bushes.

Alice stared in wonder at the words she now saw, painted on to the wall in bright red paint and tall letters.

ALWAYS BE PREPARED.

And in the middle of it all, next to a home-made cup and a very old book of some kind, there was a bed. It was made from two old tree trunks, and covered in huge, wide leaves.

And under those leaves was a shape.

A slowly moving shape. Rising and falling.

A snoring shape.

20

DAYS UNTIL ARRIVAL: 774
I'M KIDDING. IT'S 3.

Lydia woke in a panic.

'BAAAAAH!' she shrieked, terrified.

'BAAAAAAH!' yelled the kids, now just as terrified.

The old lady shot out of her rickety bed.

'INTRUDERS!' she yelled, leaping into a karate pose. 'What are you? Who are you? What's your favourite colour?'

She wouldn't keep still. Her mind seemed to be racing at a million miles an hour as she ran her hands through her hair and tried to make sense of things. Hamish noticed the thick white stripe that ran through it.

'What are you, spies?' she said. 'Why is there a unicorn? Who sent you? Is it teatime? You look like small humans. What are they called again? Think, Lydia, *think*. Stinkers? No! *Kids*!'

'Yes!' said Hamish, pleased to help. 'We're kids!'

'Aha! IT SPEAKS!' said Lydia. 'Then prepare for a quick test! What famous city am I thinking of?'

'Uh, how am I supposed to know that?' said Hamish.

'CORRECT!' she said. 'Who wants a coconut? What day is it, Wednesday?'

Hamish cast an eye to Alice. He couldn't help but feel that Lydia might be a little bit . . . mad. Sitting on her own in a cave for years and years had obviously not been good for her.

Alice was staring at Lydia, a great big smile beaming across her face.

'I can't BELIEVE we FOUND you!' she said, and her eyes might as well have been heart-shaped.

'I can't BELIEVE I've been FOUND!' replied Lydia. 'I gave up hope years ago! And yet somewhere out there, someone was looking for me! Never ceasing their quest! Always searching! Relentlessly! Tell me, child, how long have you been looking for me?'

'In all honesty, about twenty-four hours,' said Alice.

'Oh.'

'But Kit here has been at it a lot longer!'

'You look familiar,' said Lydia, looking at Kit. 'In fact, you all look a little familiar. If a bit odd.'

'I am Kit Alexander Lopez from Monster Patrol,' said Kit, a little hurt. Hamish noticed. He saw that underneath all the bravado and shouting, really Kit lacked a little confidence.

'Monster Patrol?' she said, surprised, and studying the logo on Kit's plumber/boiler suit. 'But . . . but you're a child! Why would Monster Patrol send a child?'

'My grandmamma entrusted me with the quest to keep looking for you once she had passed. Monster Patrol needs you.'

'Your grandmamma?' asked Lydia. 'Wait . . . you said your name is Lopez?'

'My grandmamma was Luciana,' said Kit, nervously.

Lydia turned away. She stared at the wall for a few seconds, thinking of her old friend. The many adventures they'd shared. How much they loved each other.

'So she never gave up on me,' she whispered.

'*Never*,' said Kit, feeling so proud. 'And nor would I.'

From somewhere outside the cave there came a noise.

Birds were taking flight from trees!

They shot past the sun. The shadows flashed across the clearing.

Lydia, being someone who knew the value of pulling yourself together, took a deep breath and turned back to face the children.

'Be prepared!' she said, her eyes darting nervously around. 'The BÜÜÜÜG could return at any second!'

'So how big exactly is this thing?' asked Hamish, nervously, and Lydia realised she still had no idea who the boy with the unicorn was, or the strangely quiet girl at his side.

'What's the story with you two?' said Lydia, spinning round and pointing at Hamish and

Alice. 'Spill the beans, bozos!'

Alice suddenly felt shy. She didn't know how to handle this. Or what a bozo was. She wanted to fling herself at her grandma, but Lydia seemed so tough and no-nonsense. Alice didn't want to make a fool of herself.

'I'm Hamish, and this is my best friend Alice,' said Hamish, taking charge. 'We're from a town called Starkley and we need your help.'

Lydia gasped.

'Starkley?' she said. 'I remember that name!'

'It's in real trouble. You're the biggest monster expert in the world, and it looks like there's a pretty big monster headed our way.'

'Starkley,' said Lydia, to herself. 'Then they did it. Then they went ahead with the experiment . . . What did you say your names were?'

'Hamish Ellerby,' said Hamish.

'And Alice,' said Alice. 'Alice Shepherd.'

Lydia stared at the girl before her.

Alice *Shepherd*?

From *Starkley*?

She studied the big eyes, her determined face. She noticed her cherry red army boots, her ALWAYS BE PREPARED badge, the blue stripe in her hair.

She broke into a huge smile, opened up her arms, and just as she was about to launch herself at Alice . . .

BVVVVVVVVVVVVVVVVV!

It sounded like the flight of a million billion bees.

It sounded like it had the power of a thousand jet planes.

It sounded like fifty of your dads, all snoring at once.

Something was coming. Squeezing its way through one of the tunnels on the way to Lydia's tropical jail cell.

'We can catch up on the way,' said Lydia. 'But right now we need to be anywhere in the world other than here.'

The noise grew. Dust began to fall from the ceiling, as the vibration of the BVVVV shifted the very foundations of the room. Uni bridled, nervously. And for good reason.

'The BÜÜÜÜG!' cried Lydia. 'My dreaded captor!'

How would the beastly BÜÜÜÜG react to a bunch of strangers?

And to its prize catch trying to escape?

IN.

IT.

CAME!

21

DAYS UNTIL ARRIVAL: NEVER MIND THAT, WE HAVE A MUCH MORE IMMEDIATE PROBLEM!

'Run, children! Save yourselves!'

yelled Lydia. 'I am old! I have lived my life! For too long I have been captured by this thing! Kept in a cave, behind his web of steel! Today I will fight to the death!'

Lydia had tried to escape in the past, of course, using all her monster hunting knowledge. She'd knitted ropes from vines, she'd crafted booby-traps from coconuts, she'd even written a number of inspiring poems to try and win it over...but the BÜÜÜÜG had avoided all her efforts (especially her poems) until she'd been forced to accept her fate.

Hamish, Alice and Kit were panicking, ready for the dreadful BÜÜÜÜG to show itself. They could hear it. They could feel it. They could sense it. But where was it?

Uni was tense and alert, his eyes like steel now, his teeth bared – he could sense a fight was in the air. He dipped his head, ready to use his tusk, but no matter how fearsome he made himself look, he could not hide his own fear.

'**BÜÜÜÜG!**' yelled Lydia, as more dust fell and brown clouds wisped around her. 'Come get me!'

The old lady stood in the well of sunlight, brightly lit, her fists out like a boxer. The **BÜÜÜÜG** had to be circling in the gloom around her because its horrible noise bounced from the walls. It was like it was everywhere and nowhere at the same time.

Hamish squinted into the darkness as he tried to catch a glimpse of this awful monster.

And then . . .

'**AHA!**' yelled Lydia. '**BEHOLD!**' Hamish blinked.

Hovering right in front of Lydia was something both Hamish and Alice recognised from her monster book. It was indeed THE **BÜÜÜÜG**!

The only surprise was that it was about the size of a jelly baby.

'*That's* the **BÜÜÜÜG**?' said Alice, almost

offended. 'It's like being terrorised by a coffee bean!'

'Don't underestimate it,' said Kit. 'It can spin a web in a hot second. It can shoot its poison, and it can scratch, and its strength knows no bounds. It can live up to a thousand years, because it's a survivor, a psychopath, a cold-blooded killer! It captures and keeps it prey, until it is ready and ripe to eat! It has more power than you would ever imagine!'

Alice stared at it with a new wonder. She knew Kit was right, you must never underestimate an enemy.

And now the tiny BÜÜÜÜG was hovering directly

in front of Lydia's nose. It looked like it was preparing for something. A sting? A bite?

It began to shake.

And vibrate.

And the noise grew.

And grew.

The **BVVVVVV** shook the very cave to its rafters.

A coconut tree fell over! Lydia's cups and plates rattled on her home-made shelves. A chunk of the cave fell from the ceiling, and dust POFFED into the air, right where poor Uni was standing . . .

Uni shook his head, trying to get rid of the cloud of dust so he could concentrate, but that was the very worst thing to do, because now it was right up his nostrils!

Uni sputtered and spluttered. His nostrils flared. Hamish had had enough colds and had accidentally over-peppered enough eggs to know what was about to happen!

Wait! *He knew what was about to happen*!

Quickly, Hamish clambered on to Uni's back, and used both his hands to direct the unicorn's head. Uni tried to resist, but Hamish remained strong, pointing the unicorn's head towards the BÜÜÜÜG and—

'BLACHOOOOFFFFF!'

The unicorn sneezed powerfully from the dust!

But this wasn't just a sneeze.

This was a *unicorn* sneeze!

A great WOFF of FIRE shot from its nostrils, like a flamethrower!

The whole cave lit up. The sheer heat made everyone feel like they were blushing. Uni smiled a nervous 'sorry!'.

And then everyone noticed the noise had stopped.

Hamish looked at the BÜÜÜÜG.

It was hanging in the air still.

But it was black.

And a small wisp of smoke twirled into the air above it.

It dropped to the floor with a PIFF and then POFF – crumbled to dust.

Thanks to Hamish, the fireball missed Lydia by millimetres and hit his target exactly!

'Well, I wish I'd tried something like that before,' said Lydia, gathering together a few of her things, and reaching down to pick up the old book by her bed. 'Now let's get out of here!'

22

DAYS UNTIL ARRIVAL:
2-AND-A-HALF!

By the time the group made it back to the ravine, Smasha was landing the Astral Plane. When Alice and Kit hadn't been where he'd left them, he'd circled over the jungle trying to spot them with his heat-seekers.

'A Puffox!' yelled Lydia over the noise and wind from the engines, and pointing in panic at the monster at the wheel. 'I'll handle this! The best way to dispatch a Puffox is six hard tugs to the tail! Weakens their knees. After that, a couple of bops to the ribs and he'll be Puffox putty in my hands!'

Lydia got ready to fight, but Kit leapt in front of her.

'He's my Familiar! Monster Patrol pairs up kids and monsters these days!'

'Kids and monsters?' said Lydia, her horror turning to delight. 'So you're telling me that all over the world, while

I was stuck in a cave for decades, there were hundreds of teams of monsters and kids teaming up to battle evil?'

Kit looked sheepish.

'Well . . . to be honest . . . it's just me and Smasha. Ever since Grandmamma died . . . things have been a little harder.'

Lydia's face softened as she watched the plane doors open. 'That could do with a lick of paint, too.'

Hamish turned to Uni. He couldn't very well take the unicorn all the way back to Starkley, but Hamish was worried about leaving Uni here. After all, he'd helped distract the other unicorns. They would not appreciate that one bit.

'Can we make a stop on the way?' he asked Kit. 'I think someone deserves a treat.'

After they'd dropped Uni at Hotel Empanada – and told a *delighted* Brendon that this unicorn was a hero and was his new permanent companion and deserved all the cactus sugar cubes he could find – Hamish hit VIDEO CALL on the dashboard to check in on the **PDF**.

'Hamish! We've been waiting for your call!' said Elliot, live from Garage 5, staring into the camera in his computer.

'We're in the Amazon rainforest!' said Hamish.

'Of course you are,' said Elliot. 'I reckoned you would either still be in the Amazon rainforest, or at Frinkley leisure centre because it's 2-for-1 on hotdogs today.'

In the background, Hamish could hear the Central Speaker honking away.

'What's happening there?'

'What's *not* happening, H?' Buster said, leaning into view. 'The curfew's earlier. They're bringing down the barriers around Starkley. We're on Hot Alert.'

'Why?' said Alice.

'Because whatever's on that radar has sped up,' said Clover, peering in. 'It's like in the last day or so, it's realised it needs to get here quicker. **Belasko**'s going nutso! This monster might be a total *cycle path*!'

The only thing that had changed in the last day was that Hamish and Alice had found Lydia. Could that be connected?

'Well, we're on our way back to Starkley,' said Hamish, as Smasha powered the boosters and the Astral Plane shot through the sky. 'And tell **Belasko** – we're bringing Lydia!'

'Starkley,' said Lydia, quietly, as Hamish hung up the call.

'I can't believe that worked out.'

Alice turned to her.

'What do you mean?' she said.

And so Lydia explained.

'In 1982, **Belasko** built Starkley. A town designed to be so boring that no one would ever want to investigate any further. But a town that would hide a secret,' Lydia began.

'Yes,' said Alice. 'We know the secret now. You press a button in the town clock and the whole place turns into Earth's best chance of defence against evil. Buildings turn into control rooms, that sort of thing. Hamish's dad is actually a top agent there.'

'Yeah,' said Hamish. 'We go on, like, missions together and stuff. Or we will.'

Lydia smiled, as if none of this surprised her one bit.

'Ah, but there was another purpose behind Starkley,' she said. 'An even larger one. To do with the people who would live there. **Belasko** made sure that it was appealing to a certain type of person. They would offer them cheap houses, make sure there were good schools . . .'

'What type of people?' asked Hamish.

'Useful people,' she said. 'Some young **Belasko** agents.

People who might have talents in their family heritage. People who could look at the world differently. People with adventure, or brains, or fearlessness in their bloodlines. People who might rise to the occasion, whatever the occasion is.'

'That sounds mad,' said Hamish.

'And yet here you all are,' said Lydia. 'Hiding in plain sight. You, your friends . . . people like my daughter . . .'

'Does your . . . daughter . . . have special skills?' said Alice, cagily. She wasn't quite sure how to tell Lydia exactly who she was yet.

Lydia traced her finger down the stripe in Alice's hair.

'Some things run in the family,' she said.

Alice looked up at the old lady with the white stripe in her hair. Lydia nodded towards Hamish.

'It's no coincidence that the son of a top **Belasko** agent might become friends with a girl like you, Alice.'

'So you know who I am?' she said, as Lydia took her hand.

Lydia squeezed it.

'Of course I do,' she said. 'Second I saw you. And you are proof the experiment worked. I'm very proud. Tell me about the friends at home I saw.'

'Well, there's Elliot,' she said. 'He was the first on screen.

He's the one who first noticed your HELP ME message in the paper.'

'A natural codebreaker,' she said. 'You see, I knew They were after me.'

'They?' said Hamish, but he had a feeling he knew who she meant. The Superiors. The awful alien race they had come up against before. The ones that had taken his uncle to their heart and made him evil.

'I knew I could be facing a trap, going into the jungle on my own like that. But I was blinded by ambition. I had been scared off by a monster, and if the enemy saw I could be scared, they would see a weakness. I had to show I would not back down. The night I got there I realised there was no way out. If I returned home, they would send spies to follow me, and I would lead them straight to your mother.'

'The Superiors?' said Alice, and Lydia nodded.

'But if they caught me, at least I had sent the diary somewhere safe, where my clues might be discovered. It was like calling for backup. I'm looking forward to thanking Elliot.'

'The other boy was Buster,' said Alice. 'He's great with gadgets and mechanics, he set up our whole base. And then there's Clover, she's a master of disguise.'

'It seems they all have special skills,' said Lydia.

'Well, there's Venk, too,' said Alice. 'We're still working his skills out.'

'Did you ever find that convenient?' asked Lydia. 'The fact that your friends all excel at certain things?'

Alice looked confused. What was Lydia saying?

But it started to hit her. Could it really be coincidence that a gang like the **PDF** had found each other, completely by *chance*?

That they would all have been brought up in a town like Starkley?

That they were all about the *same age*?

'Starkley was an investment in Earth's future,' said Lydia. 'It was exciting times in what we called the Union. **Belasko** and Monster Patrol often worked together. Of course, as we faced greater threats, our power was weakened . . . which is why we needed to keep the future of our organisation safe and hidden in plain sight.'

Lydia opened the book she'd brought with her from the cave. It was old, creased and leather-bound. It looked like a book of spells or something.

'This is Luciana's book of dreams,' she said, and Kit

gasped from the cockpit. He had heard these stories from his grandmamma. But he thought her book had been lost. It had disappeared along with Lydia. 'I have had many years to study them, as you can imagine. She believed that dreams held the secrets of our futures. I once thought that was nonsense, to be honest, but she seemed to get things right a lot.'

Kit smiled.

'Anyway, one of Luciana's dreams told her that our planet's worst threat would appear in a small town. A man with great power. An apprentice of the Superiors, keen to make his name.'

'Scarmarsh,' said Hamish and Alice in unison.

Lydia's eyes widened.

'He was the second-worst villain in the universe,' said Alice. 'But now we reckon he's top of the league!'

'Luciana said that the danger would come from the sea,' said Lydia, darkly, 'but a boy on the cliffs would hold the secret to beating it.'

'I told you, Alice!' said Kit.

'That boy would know the mind of the monster,' said Lydia. 'He would be the Chosen One.'

Alice looked at Hamish as his own dream flashed through

his mind again. The moment of responsibility was not lost on him.

And suddenly he felt a little sick.

In many ways, he knew he was already the Chosen One. Scarmarsh was choosing him. So, while he didn't know the mind of the monster, a monster certainly seemed to know Hamish's mind.

He wanted to say something. He wanted desperately to be rid of this secret. But he couldn't find the words. Not now. Not when they seemed to believe in him so much.

Lydia squeezed Alice's hand again, as the Astral Plane banked left and began to whizz over the ocean.

'You know that when we get back, there's someone you're going to have to say sorry to almost immediately,' said Alice.

'I know,' said Lydia, sadly. 'I imagine your mum is quite angry with me, disappearing like that. I suppose I was always disappearing. But it was my calling. I regret it, of course. I thought of her every day I was there. I wished I'd been around more. I wondered what her life was like. I wondered if someone like you existed. I'm so pleased you do.'

Alice smiled.

'Now!' said Lydia, eager to get stuck in. 'What can you tell me about this sea monster?'

Lydia grinned. She'd been waiting *forever* for this.

23

DAYS UNTIL ARRIVAL: 2

The **PDF** was ready and waiting with a full briefing as the gang poured out of the Astral Plane and into Garage 5.

Dozens of people had rushed to see the return of this mysterious craft as they heard it tear through the clouds.

The second it touched down, Kit opened the doors and yelled, 'I am Kit Alexander Lopez of Monster Patrol! And I return your crazy people!'

Hamish's mum had been at the front of the crowd, wanting to make sure he was safe. She knew she had to get used to her son's increasing role in protecting the world, but still – you don't go running off to the Amazon rainforest willy-nilly. Madame Cous Cous had polished her glasses so she could get an extra special good look.

Belasko had requested an immediate meeting with Lydia, but she was very firm as she stepped out: she would be working with the **PDF** first and foremost. They were welcome to join, but after all, it was the **PDF** who had found the clues, travelled all that way *and* rescued her. Where had **Belasko** been? No, she wanted the **PDF** in charge!

KNOW YOUR ENEMY

TERRIBLES

Elliot had prepared a full briefing around the table. Also some squash.

The sea monster was indeed moving faster, he said, but they had allowed for that. If it continued at this speed, the experts said it would hit Starkley at around 9 p.m., just two days from now.

KNOW YOUR ENEMY

SPYTRAP

Two days was *nothing*!

And, what's more, it was bigger. Much bigger. They could tell by the pace that it wasn't swimming. It was walking. Meaning it had legs. And if it had legs, that meant it could walk on land.

But even though Lydia should have been completely focused on Elliot's intel, she was enthralled by what was on the walls.

'Oh, my!' she said, pushing Venk out of the way to stare at the **PDF**'s KNOW YOUR ENEMY! posters. '*Monstrum horrendum!*'

She moved from one poster to the other, giving each monster its proper scientific title.

'*Bestia terribilis!*' she almost yelled, pointing at a picture of a Terrible. 'I recognise the markings! Strangely beautiful! But these were only ever a rumour . . . Unless a particular someone perfected the formula?'

'Scarmarsh!' said Clover. 'They're called Terribles. He's quite good at this stuff.'

'*Venus exploratorem captionem,*' said Kit, staring at a picture of a Venus spytrap, his arms behind his back, absolutely fascinated.

'Extraordinary!' said Lydia. 'And you have battled with these things?'

'Yup!' said Alice. 'It's pretty much what we do. That, and homework.'

'You see?' said Lydia. 'Monster hunting runs in the family. Just as so many other things do. Buster, Alice tells me that you're a technical whizz?'

'Me?' said Buster, shyly. 'I used to sit in the garage with my dad. He would let me tinker with things. Let me use his spanners whenever I liked. He was pretty brilliant at that stuff.'

'And Clover – you have quite a way with disguises?'

Clover laughed.

'My mum used to pretend my grandad was an amazing spy, codenamed The Blender, because he could blend in to any situation. Cowboy. Camel. Marine biologist. You'd never know he was there. Until he said "hello, I'm a cowboy, camel, marine biologist". That's why they could never throw him a surprise party. My mum says it would usually turn out he was already in the room, disguised as a lamp! But she was just joking.'

'What if she *wasn't*?' said Lydia, mysteriously. 'And you . . . *Hamish*.'

Hamish looked embarrassed.

'No prizes for guessing what runs in your family's blood,' she said, placing a hand on his shoulder.

Wait! Did Lydia know the truth? Did she know that he was related to Scarmarsh?

'Heroism!' said Lydia.

Hamish could not take this any longer. All the guilt. And

now this Chosen One and *heroism* stuff. You know when you have a secret and it's just bursting to come out? Something that weighs so heavily on your shoulders that you think you'll never have the strength to lift it? Something you need to share, but you're too scared to? Hamish needed to say something, and now was the time.

'It's true that my dad is a top **Belasko** agent,' said Hamish. 'But there's something else. Something I haven't told any of you about, because I was too worried you'd be scared of me or kick me out of the **PDF** or something.'

His friends all swapped confused glances. What could possibly be so bad they'd kick Hamish out of the gang?! Wait – had he been stealing Chomps or something?

Hamish took a deep breath.

'Axel Scarmarsh is my uncle.'

There was complete silence. Lydia took a step back. Hamish looked up at his friends, who seemed completely blindsided.

'*Scarmarsh*?' said Buster. 'Is this a joke?'

'No. My dad is his brother,' said Hamish, lowering his head.

'Yin and yang,' said Lydia, shaking her head. 'Good and evil.'

'Hamish,' said Venk. 'Why didn't you tell us?'

'It scares me,' admitted Hamish. 'I feel responsible. All this time he's been attacking Starkley. He seemed to have some kind of vendetta against it but we could never work out why. And when I found out, I worried he was choosing Starkley to attack because of Dad. But now I think it's because of me.'

'But he captured us once,' said Alice. 'Why wouldn't he just have kept you?'

'I think he's changed his plans and decided he wants something from me. Maybe he's realised he'll never beat my dad or turn him evil. But maybe he thinks he has a better chance with me. And what would hurt my dad more than that?'

'Has he told you this?' asked Kit, folding his arms, curious.

'He comes to me in dreams,' admitted Hamish. 'I *think*. I mean, maybe they're just dreams. But they seem real. Am I going mad?'

Lydia shook her head, but had no time to reassure him. She needed to know more about the dreams, and fast.

'They usually start on a cliff,' said Hamish. 'The whole **PDF** is there. But I'm gripped by an impossible force and can't move.'

'The Chosen One,' said Lydia, in awe. 'The boy on the cliffs! Kit – get the book.'

Kit dashed out of the room to fetch Luciana's book from the Astral Plane. Maybe there were more clues in there.

'Hamish,' said Lydia, sensing what Hamish was thinking. 'Right now, you need to know two things.'

'What are they?' said Hamish, quivering, hoping that they were two *good* things.

'Number one,' she said. 'You are *not* your uncle.'

'And number two?'

'That might be the key to beating him.'

Suddenly, the door flung open.

'GUYS!' came a voice.

It was Grenville Bile. Well, just look at his El Gamba costume. Desperate to distract herself from the thought of the sea monster, Clover had obviously been working on it right up until the world had turned into one big emergency. Grenville had gone full prawn. There were googly bug eyes strapped to the top of his mask. Dangly legs woven into a pink cape. A couple of droopy antennae.

'TELL ME YOU BROUGHT MY PRAWN BURRITO?' he yelled.

24

DAYS UNTIL ARRIVAL: 2

Alice held Lydia's hand as they walked to Viola Road. She'd left Kit in charge of briefing the **PDF** further, but she had one very important question that simply couldn't wait.

'Who was that odd child dressed as a crustacean?' she asked.

'Grenville,' said Alice. 'He's okay once you get used to him. I think he's going mad because there's no fast food in town any more. He hasn't had a burger in weeks. He's had to start eating broccoli. It's really getting to him.'

'Well,' said Lydia. 'I suppose you can't all be geniuses.'

They stopped outside Alice's house.

'This is it,' she told Lydia.

After they went inside, Alice made her grandma wait in the hallway. She could hear her mum in the kitchen, chopping stuff. That's what she did when she was worried.

'Mum,' said Alice, and her mum spun round.

'ALICE!'

Alice braced herself. She hadn't even left her mum a note

before jumping in a spaceship and shooting off to the Amazon. She reckoned her mum must have been furious when she'd found out.

But her mum didn't seem angry. She seemed entirely relieved.

'Hamish's dad explained everything to me. About Monster Patrol. About my mum. She was captured, wasn't she?'

Alice nodded. 'She was trying to keep the world a little safer. It's just in her. She says it runs in the family, trying to save the world.'

'You're *my* world,' said Alice's mum. 'It's *my* job to keep *you* safe. That's what she taught me, though I don't think she meant to.' Then something dawned on her. 'Wait, what do you mean she says it runs in the family?'

'Uh, about that,' said Alice, and she walked towards the door and opened it. Standing there was Lydia.

'Mum?' said Alice's mum.

'Sorry I'm late, darling,' said Lydia. 'I got a little . . . bugged down at work.'

And Alice's heart swelled as her mum and grandma ran to each other and melted into each other's arms.

And, as they hugged, Alice's mum reached out to squeeze her brave, brave daughter's hand.

Hamish paced up and down. There was a lot on his mind.

Lydia had spoken quickly and with great purpose at a town meeting later that evening.

It was her professional opinion, she told them, that whatever monster was headed towards Starkley was coming to destroy it once and for all. She had asked the **PDF** to fill her and Kit in on the history of the town, and the very strange things that had been happening.

Like the WorldStoppers, who had attempted to pause time itself in order to steal the grown-ups. The Venus Spytraps that had littered the town, snapping at people with their ginormous jaws. The Hypnobots that had attempted to zap the world to turn it stupid. The GravityBurps that had sent everyone high into the air, and the weird hypnotised babies that had risen up against them.

And, of course, the Terribles. The monsters that had once been just a madman's idea, but which Scarmarsh had developed and perfected on the island of Frykt.

'Don't underestimate the Terribles and their part in this!' she declared, standing on top of the Astral Plane parked in the middle of town, looking out at the citizens who had chosen to remain. 'I am certain they will play their role!'

'How do you know?' asked Mr Slackjaw, who'd loaned her his ladder so she could clamber up the side of the plane.

'Well, what normally follows a battering ram?' she said. 'After it's knocked down the door to the castle?'

Everyone looked blank.

'Foot soldiers!' yelled Kit.

'And what normally follows a Trojan horse, once it's made its way to the very heart of its target?' asked Lydia.

Everyone looked blank.

'Foot soldiers!' yelled Kit.

'What I'm saying is, whatever this thing is, that won't be the end of it. The monster that's coming will cause terror and division! But what comes after will do the real work!'

'Terribles,' said Hamish, and Kit nodded gravely.

'So we have to do what we can to stop the big thing.

I propose a quick training session in the art of Monster Patrolling for the entire town. Kit, Smasha and I will make sure that the people of Starkley are well prepared for whatever this thing actually turns out to be. Serpent. Sea-Ape. Mega Bug.'

She pointed at Hamish.

'And we will keep the Chosen One close by and protected!'

Hamish blushed. He wasn't really into being called the Chosen One all the time. Imagine if that was how you were introduced all the time by your parents. 'These are our children Sam and Sarah, and that one over there in

MONSTER PATROLLING
Including 'Footprint Spotting', 'Binocular Work', 'Dealing with Micromonsters', 'Scales, Whales and Fails' and 'How to Run Away'.

KIT ALEXANDER

the corner is the Chosen One.' Or imagine if your teacher called you that when they did the register? *'Joe ... Amit ... Jade ... Mo ... the Chosen One?'* You'd get sick of it pretty quickly. Anyway, Hamish decided he just had to go along with it, because that's what a Chosen One would do, and maybe that's why he'd been chosen.

And so while Alice's mum handed out sandwiches, Kit and Smasha set up their training camp in the middle of the town square, and set to work ...

LOPEZ PRESENTS

MONSTER IDENTIFICATION
Including 'Slime Analysis', 'Basics of Beast DNA', 'How to Get That Slime Off Your Fingers', and 'How to Run Away, Module 2'.

MONSTER COMBAT
'Foot stamps and knee kicks!', 'How to Inflate Your Head to Three Times Its Normal Size!', 'Shooting Poison Darts Out of Your Face!', 'Identifying a weak spot and exploiting it!', Plus! 'How to Run Away, Module 3'.

'Well, at least we're preparing!' said Hamish to Lydia, feeling better, as he watched some of the grown-ups doing their synchronised foot stamps and lunges with Smasha. 'Though I'm not sure how I'm supposed to inflate my own head. Still, Frau Fussbundler's knee kick looks pretty awesome!'

Lydia smiled, and took Hamish to one side.

'Oh, my boy, Kit is not doing this to prepare the town,' she said. 'This is to distract it.'

She sat Hamish down on the bench to explain more.

'Sometimes, when you face a great threat, you need to feel you are doing something, even when you are small and helpless. Starkley won't be saved by knee kicks. Or even by missiles.'

Behind them, the great old town clock rose and grew. The ground rumbled as a new section broke through the earth underneath.

With a CLUNK, pistons started to whirr, and the clock was angled into position.

It now looked like the missile it was always designed to be. The centrepiece of the town might also be the centrepiece of the battle, should it come to that.

'It's important that people feel they are doing something

to protect the town. They need to feel unified. Especially when Starkley has been shut off from the rest of the country.'

That really narked Hamish. Think of all the times they'd saved the world. And what was their reward? The Prime Minister cutting them off and leaving the **PDF** and **Belasko** to deal with things while they just looked the other way and hoped for the best.

'No,' said Lydia, 'what we need to do is see if we can work out from Luciana's book what it is that makes *you* the Chosen One. Because clearly, you and this monster have some kind of connection.'

Hamish looked up into her eyes.

'But what's going to happen when it gets here?' he asked.

Neither of them knew.

And that scared poor Hamish Ellerby.

25

HOURS UNTIL ARRIVAL: 48

Lydia had gone to brief **Belasko** on '*Creatures of the Deep – 1890 to the Present Day*', the follow-up to her hit lecture '*Monsters on the Seafood Diet – they see food, they eat it!*', which was a joke first told in Ancient Greece.

She wanted to impart all the information she could so that everyone might know what to expect when whatever this monster was finally appeared. Only when it appeared would they know what course of action to take. Could they reason with it? Could they distract it? Could they trick it?

Or would they have to fight it?

She'd compared notes with Kit – who loved talking with a proper monster expert – and even got a monster's perspective from Smasha. After that, Lydia set the **PDF** their important tasks.

Buster was to research any technology he thought might be useful for a water-based monster. Cannons! Barriers! Big metal nets! **Belasko** were going to get him whatever materials he needed and he was allowed to use any spanner he liked!

Elliot was given direct access to the radar room, so he could work alongside the **Belasko** agents keeping a keen eye on the dot's movement as it got closer to Starkley, while also researching possible sea monsters.

Clover was going to be given a crash course in modern-day spy techniques by a team of **Belasko** agents. If spying ran in her family, it was important she was helped to reach her full potential!

Venk was put in charge of sandwiches.

And Hamish? Well, Lydia said Hamish needed to just talk. Sometimes, she said, talking about whatever was on your mind was a great way to discover what was *really* on your mind. She told him he needed to stop being quiet about his feelings, and just let them pour out, like a big gushing river. Luciana's dream had convinced everyone that Hamish might well be the key to all this.

He took her advice to heart and decided to have a chat with Alice to try and work things out in his mind and see if she had any idea why Hamish Ellerby of 13 Lovelock Close might in fact be humanity's Chosen One.

'You just need to think, Hamish!' said Alice, which actually wasn't the helpful insight that Hamish had been hoping for.

'I *have* been thinking!' he replied. 'I just don't understand it. I don't have any special connections with monsters. On the whole, I dislike them!'

They were wandering the empty streets of Starkley at dusk. It was after the curfew, of course, when kids were supposed to be indoors, but Lydia had insisted that Hamish and Alice be given the freedom to think and talk.

They passed Lord of the Fries and sighed.

STILL NO CHIPS read the sign. OR FISH EITHER, ACTUALLY.

Hamish looked at the menu. Everything had been crossed out. There were no sausages. No mushy peas. No curry sauce. Not even any cheap scampi.

His tummy rumbled. He'd love some cheap scampi again.

'Maybe it's not a normal monster?' said Alice, still thinking. 'Maybe it's a monster that means something to you? Maybe it's something you love, or fear? Grandma Lydia seems pretty sure it *must* be *something*.'

'But what am I supposed to do when it gets here?' asked Hamish. 'What does a Chosen One *do*?'

Alice looked like she wanted to help him, but just didn't know how. Hamish felt the same. He hadn't asked to be the Chosen One. He hadn't asked for these dreams. He hadn't asked to be the nephew of the universe's second-worst supervillain. Sometimes he just wanted to sit in his pants watching the telly.

When he really thought about it, he felt that Lydia had been telling the **PDF** that they were all Chosen Ones, in a way. That Buster had his technical ability for a reason. That Clover may very well *really* have had a grandad called The Blender. That perhaps everybody has a reason they'd been born here, or led here, and a reason they'd come together. Still – it felt like Hamish had been given the biggest job, and it was one he'd have to live up to.

'Tell me about the dreams again,' said Alice.

'They come and go,' said Hamish. 'At first they were always the same. And then they started to change.'

Alice had an idea.

'Then you need to have another one,' she said.

'But I don't want to have them at all,' said Hamish.

'Hamish,' she said. 'This thing – whatever it is – is going to destroy Starkley. In just two days. You and I both know it. I hear the grown-ups whispering. I think my mum's been talking to your mum about moving house at the last minute. We'd have to go and stay with my cousin, two hundred miles away.'

Hamish was pretty sure his parents would have a backup plan too, if it all got too dangerous. One that meant never coming back to Starkley. Losing his friends.

Alice clapped her hands together and made an only-one-thing-for-it face.

'You need to start using your dream properly,' she said.

'Using my dream?' Hamish replied.

'Yes. Luciana told Kit that some people can dream differently,' said Alice. 'In all the dreams you've told me about, things happen to you. Everything happens to you. And Scarmarsh talks to you.'

'So?' said Hamish.

'So what if you took *control of your dream*?' she said, and Hamish's eyes widened in fear.

Because how was he supposed to do that?

𝖶

That night, in bed, Hamish stared at the ceiling.

He didn't want to go to sleep.

He didn't want to lose control again.

And he didn't know how to *take* control.

He could see through his curtains that, outside, the street lights were flashing red and blue. Every now and again he'd hear the honk of the Central Speaker.

He lay there, for what could have been an hour, or it could have been eternity, until moment by moment his eyelids grew heavy and he seemed to fall backwards into a tunnel, finally finding an exhausted sleep . . .

THE DREAM

No Central Speaker.

No flashing lights.

Silence. Blackness. Nothing.

None of the normal night sounds, invading the dream. No burble of the telly downstairs. No cutlery being put away in drawers. No dishwasher being opened. No quiet mumbling of Jimmy in the room next door, composing his latest terrible poem.

Just silence . . . followed by the sound of a key rattling around in a lock.

Hamish sees nothing, not at first.

But he feels where he is. He is on a hard wooden chair. The room he'd been in last time.

The key rattles again. He sits up, tense.

There is only the sound; there is nothing to look at. A complete absence of anything. Like being in space, in a galaxy with no stars.

The rattling stops, as the key finds its mark.

Every tooth of the key clicks as its blade slides into the lock.

Hamish hears each spring-loaded pin line up with the next.

And then the key turns and the lock clicks . . .

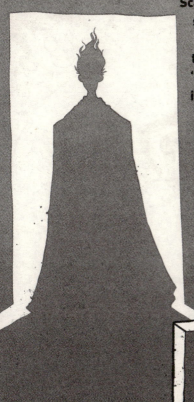

the doorway – a familiar figure.

'Where do you think you are?' says Scarmarsh, quite calmly.

Hamish shakes his head. He doesn't know. He wants to stand up to Scarmarsh, but he can't yet find the strength.

'Perhaps you think you're still over the ocean,' Scarmarsh continues. 'Maybe you think you're safe at home in bed.'

Hamish feels himself prickle with sweat and fear.

'But it's not about where *you* are, Hamish. It's about where *I* am.'

'And where are you?' replies Hamish, finally finding his voice.

But had he chosen to say that? Or had the dream made him do it?

'I'm here,' says Scarmarsh, tapping his temple with one finger. 'I am in your mind.'

He claps his hands together and Hamish flinches.

'The power of a child's imagination is immense,' says Scarmarsh. 'They think differently. I can conjure up your greatest hopes. The things you love . . .'

Around Hamish, suddenly . . . images, feelings, memories . . . the sound of a river, and walking with his dad, and his brother Jimmy up ahead laughing and flinging a Frisbee. The smells of his grandparents' house in Scotland, the smell of Mum's sausage and mash, her hand smoothing down his hair as he drifts off to sleep . . . good feelings. Safe feelings. Happy ones.

'But I can also conjure up . . . your *fears*.'

And in one quick and jolting burst, the black walls fall away and Hamish is sucked into the air – chair and all! – where a violent storm begins to rage around him.

He is soaking wet now, the deafening roar of wind whipping around him, as the same storm he'd dreamt of so many times hurled high waves beneath him.

But Hamish has some fight in him. '**I . . . WILL . . . TAKE . . . CONTROL!**' he shouts, into the wind, his words carried off so that he can barely hear them himself.

'**I WILL TAKE CONTROL!**' he shouts again, and now he can move more freely . . . He'd felt like he was in jelly before, or quicksand, but now he can move his arms just like he can in real life.

But now the skies echo with the sound of an impossibly loud laugh.

BAH-HA-HA-HA-HAAA!

And down there, beneath him, Hamish sees in horror that something is rising from the depths.

The sounds it makes are like twisted metal in the seconds before a building collapses . . .

The groan of a mighty effort, the relief of a journey at an end . . .

Whatever it is, it is enormous, relentless, unstoppable . . .

He spins in the air, trying to regain control of his body.

He turns, looking back for his friends – there they are! Still standing on the cliff's edge. Looking up at him, as if he was the monster himself.

Alice.

Clover.

Elliot.

Buster.

Venk.

Kit and Smasha.

Lydia now joining them at the back, and staring up in horror.

All of them so small as to be meaningless, so hopeless in the face of this thing, this fiend, this *terror*.

But wait, he thinks, seeing *one more figure* stepping forward from between them.

The rain is fierce, and the wind buffets him around like a kite, but despite all that he can just about make out their outline.

A brave figure, in some kind of long and flapping jacket, their face obscured by something.

Who is that?

'Turn back!' screams Scarmarsh. **'LOOK AT *ME*!'**

26

DAYS UNTIL ARRIVAL: 1

'And then what happened?' asked Lydia, writing it all down and circling certain details.

'That was it,' said Hamish, shrugging. 'That was the end of the dream.'

The **PDF** all stared at him, hoping for more. Buster had closed the door of Garage 5 to make sure they had complete privacy. Most of **Belasko** had been up all night in any case, putting in flood defences and sandbags outside houses, just in case things got rather wet later on.

Hamish had asked Kit and Smasha to take the Astral Plane out for a spin over the sea, just in case they could spot any clues. He said they should take a flight over the island of Frykt – the terrifying black rock not far away that was home to the awful Terribles. Alice was still desperate to tell Hamish about Kit's secret, but knew it had to come from Kit. Alice was a person you could trust.

'Okay,' said Lydia, still focused on Hamish. 'Well, how did Scarmarsh sound when he said it? When he shouted "Look at me"?'

Hamish thought about it.

'Sort of . . . annoyed? Like I wasn't supposed to be doing what I was doing?'

The old lady smiled.

'Or maybe you weren't supposed to be seeing what you were seeing,' she said.

'Hamish, you took control of the dream, like I told you to!' said Alice. 'You spun around when you were supposed to just stare straight forward!'

'My guess is that the figure on the cliff was you, Hamish,' said Lydia. 'Dreams were more Luciana's thing, but if I'm right, you were watching through the eyes of the monster. Perhaps because you're afraid that in some way *you* are the monster. And you looked down, and you saw the forbidden truth: that you are also the Chosen One, Hamish Ellerby!'

Hamish wasn't sure what to believe. He just knew he didn't like that title.

'Or maybe it was just a dream,' said Venk, putting down another plate of home-made sandwiches.

'Elliot!' yelled Lydia. 'Where are we on sea monsters?'

Clover jumped. The **PDF** weren't used to being bossed about like this. Elliot pulled down a screen from the ceiling.

'Well, these are the most likely candidates for the Great Sea Monster of Starkley, as far as I can tell,' he said, pointing at the first picture. 'An Octo-Whale.'

'Nope,' said Lydia. 'Got rid of the last of those in the Seventies. And good riddance, I say! They were *very* windy. They don't call them "blowholes" for nothing.'

'Er . . . a MegaTurtle?' said Elliot, hopefully, pointing at the next one.

'Can't handle colder waters,' said Lydia. 'They hang out near Fiji. They like to surf on their own backs.'

'Loch Ness Monster?' said Elliot.

'Just a big worm with an even bigger ego.'

'Nuclear Piglet?'

'What's a Nuclear Piglet?'

'Dunno, I just made it up.'

'Next.'

And so Elliot kept going. Could it be the fearsome Kraken? A Japanese noseless Ningen? Could it be the enormous Leviathan? What if it was the Finfolk?

Each one was scarier than the last.

The Finfolk were an underground gang of awful Scottish

water-sorcerers.

The Hydra had loads of heads on long necks, and was the Guardian of the Underworld!

The Kraken was sometimes said to be an octopus, and sometimes a crab, and it was meant to be one of the biggest monsters the human imagination had ever dreamt up! And if Scarmarsh is somehow in control of these things, maybe people wouldn't have to dream them up any more.

'It's certainly a contender. Legend has it they can grow quickly and the bigger they get the faster they move. It may or may not have legs. I have seen one in my dreams.'

Hamish sat up, alert.

'You have dreams, too?' he said.

'I never gave up hope in that cave,' said Lydia. 'Because I would have a dream myself. The same one for years. I used to think I was simply remembering *Luciana's* dream. The one you seem to share. But perhaps I was actually seeing the same events from my own angle.'

'Were you on the cliff top in your dream?' asked Hamish. 'Wait . . . were we seeing the same thing?'

'I'd see the seas rising. I'd hear the gasps of the crowd around me. I could feel the water in the air of the cliff top. And every single time, I thought . . . it must be the Kraken.'

Alice nudged Hamish, wide-eyed.

'I always had a feeling there would be one more adventure,' said Lydia. 'If I could just wait long enough.' Her eyes shone as she stood and looked again at the pictures Elliot had found.

'I suspect we'll find out soonest,' she said. 'Well done, Elliot – our best guess is a Kraken. A giant, deadly, snapping, sucking, clawed beast of some kind. The sailor's nightmare.'

She looked almost delighted.

'Oh,' she said. 'It's so Scarmarsh it *hurts*. Now – we better check on the defences.'

Just then, the kids all sat up as they heard a roar from outside.

The Astral Plane was approaching. It must have news.

And it was coming in FAST.

27

DAYS UNTIL ARRIVAL: 1

Kit and Smasha jumped out of the plane with their arms waving in a panic outside the **PDF** HQ.

The words they were shouting were not the words anyone wanted to hear.

'IT'S HUGE!' they yelled in unison.

Hopefully they were talking about a lovely big pineapple they'd seen. Or a great new park. Or a present they'd decided to buy from a favourite local gift shop.

But no.

'We couldn't see what it was,' said Kit. 'There was a black underwater cloud made of nothing but fish! But the waves. My goodness, the waves! It seems to be bringing a storm with it. We flew right in. Thunder, lightning, wind!'

'It seemed almost to take hold of the Astral Plane itself,' said Smasha, quite shaken. 'It was like a hand plucking us out of the sky, I don't mind telling you; shaking us around, with the sheer enormous power of nature!'

Hamish knew that feeling all too well. He caught Lydia's eye. It sounded like the storm from his dreams.

'It hasn't broken the surface, whatever it is, but the waves were high and rolled around it,' said Kit. 'Fish were leaping out of the way. Seagulls were spiralling out of control. We saw a tanker batted away like it was a toy!'

The **PDF** looked *terrified*.

Just then, the Central Speaker went off, honking five times in quick succession.

'We're back on Hot Alert,' said Elliot. 'I'm going to the radar screen! It must be speeding up!'

'It's not supposed to get here till tonight!' said Buster.

'What about the Terribles?' asked Lydia, grabbing Kit. 'Did you see anything happening on their island?'

'Madam,' said Smasha, calmly, 'we felt it wasn't quite the time for sightseeing.'

'I'm willing to bet they're preparing,' said Lydia. 'I'll bet they've moved their plans up. Trying for the element of surprise! Buster, see what you can come up with!'

Buster and Clover ran for Garage 5.

'We'll need sandwiches!' yelled Venk, following after them.

'Why do you think they've changed their plans?' asked Hamish, and she leaned down to look him in the eye.

'Perhaps because Scarmarsh senses your power is growing,' she said. 'Maybe because you stood up to him in your dream. You didn't do as you were told!'

Hamish felt worse than ever. He was responsible for all this. Now it was clear to him. He *must* be the Chosen One. This couldn't just be a case of a mad uncle trying to turn him bad to punish his dad. There had to be more to it. But Hamish would never turn evil.

He wasn't his uncle's nephew – he was his dad's son.

And he wanted to be with his dad, now more than ever.

'I'll take you to your dad,' said Lydia, as if she'd read his thoughts. 'We're going to need to analyse your dream. Every little detail. Can you remember it all?'

'I think so,' said Hamish.

'Something in that last dream holds the key to this, I'm sure,' she said.

'Is this all my fault?' asked Hamish, looking to Lydia for reassurance.

'My boy,' she said. 'This is Scarmarsh's fault. No one else's. And we're going to have to tell those who don't know about your connection to him. **Belasko** is aware he's your dad's brother, of course. They just never considered that you might be in the firing line too.'

'What can I do to help?' asked Alice, urgently.

'You can come with me,' said Hamish. 'Please? I need you.'

'Always,' said Alice.

And they started to run.

28

DAYS UNTIL ARRIVAL: 0!

Hamish, Alice and Lydia jumped a barrier and found the Outdoor Command Centre.

'Dad!' yelled Hamish.

Hamish's dad looked stressed, studying the giant screen alongside Elliot. The red dot was now much larger than it had been before, and was no longer moving at a snail's pace. Not unless the snail in question had *really* been working out and also invested in rocket shoes.

Actually, snails don't have feet, forget about the shoes.

'Hamish, Elliot says you guys have a theory,' said Dad. 'You think it's a Kraken?'

'But we don't know what type. All we know is, Krakens are massive. It could be a crab, it could be an octopus, it could be anything that lives in the sea!'

Lydia stepped forward.

'The real danger here is that we get distracted,' she said.

"A monster we might be able to deal with. But hundreds of them? My theory is that Scarmarsh will unleash a mighty wave of Terribles too. An all-out assault on Starkley!'

Hamish's dad had considered that too. What if everyone had been so focused on the oncoming sea monster that they'd never thought there might be more to the plan? Sometimes when you look at the bigger picture, you miss the details. And the details can be devastating.

'**Frykt**,' said Dad, which if you'd only just picked up this book you'd assume was a swear word. 'We need a plan.'

Hamish's dad immediately started working out how many **Belasko** agents he had and what he could do with them.

'Dad,' said Hamish. 'I need to tell you something. I've been having dreams. I felt silly about them because they're just dreams, but I think they've been telling me something. This monster is big, but I think they're afraid of something. Something they didn't want me to see, but which I did anyway.'

'What is it?' said Dad, who knew these days to take Hamish's words very seriously indeed.

'It's this Chosen One thing,' said Hamish. 'Everyone seems to think it's me. And that, somehow, I can stop the monster. I'm in the air in the dream, and I look down, and I can see everyone except me, and then this figure steps out, and it *must* be me, only I can't tell because I'm in the air, so how could I see myself?'

Hamish's dad was having trouble following.

'Look, "dreams" and "spells" may be what Monster Patrol put faith in, and that's fine, but it's not the **Belasko** way—'

'Dad, I know you trust me,' interrupted Hamish. 'But can you also trust *us*?'

Hamish's dad looked at him. Then at Lydia. He was weighing everything up.

'Agent Ellerby!' came a voice, and Dad spun round.

It was Madame Cous Cous in full **Belasko** combat gear. She was pointing at the screen. It showed **Frykt** with lots of boats circling the island. Big, imposing tankers, packed with Terribles clamouring for space.

'Warships,' said Hamish's dad, realising Lydia's 'Terrible' hunch had been anything but terrible. 'We haven't got enough agents to fight two battles. We can't take care of the monster *and* stop the Terribles. We're on our own, ever since Starkley was closed off.'

'We can work together!' said Lydia. 'Like the old days of the union! **Belasko**, Monster Patrol . . . and now the **PDF**! **Belasko** can concentrate on the Terribles. And leave the monster to us.'

But Hamish's dad was having none of it.

'No way,' he said. 'Send you lot up on to a cliff to deal with it on your own?'

'We have experience with cliff-top monsters,' said Alice, remembering a certain day with a rather overbearing Venus Spytrap. 'And we've got Monster Patrol to help us!'

'One monster we might be able to handle,' said Lydia.

'But not hundreds. You take care of the Terribles, it's the only way.'

They stared at Hamish's dad while he came to a decision.

'I'm coming with you,' he said, putting on his jacket. Hamish noticed how it flapped in the wind. Wait – was his dad the mysterious figure he'd dreamt about? That figure had only appeared in the dream recently. Just when Hamish had started to discover he could control his dreams. Maybe this was a sign. A sign that you could create your own destiny. You *could* change the future.

'How long until this thing arrives?' Dad barked at an agent.

'Maybe half an hour,' she replied.

'Hamish,' he said. 'Are you sure about these dreams?'

'Dad, I am. I know it sounds weird. But weird things happen to us all the time.'

That was good enough for Angus Ellerby.

'Agent, stop those tankers,' he said. 'I'm going on a mission with my son.'

Hamish nearly burst with pride.

'We're coming too,' said Clover, skidding to a halt on her scooter, and joined by Buster, Elliot and Venk. They'd finished their meeting at HQ by voting unanimously to crack on and help Hamish as always. 'We're in the dream, after all!'

'Don't forget us,' said Kit, from behind them, as in the background, Smasha fired up the Astral Plane, ready to whisk them to the cliffs. 'We'll do whatever we can!'

Hamish knew they were but small. But they were mighty.

'And *I*,' said Venk, holding up a Tupperware box, 'have *sandwiches*.'

29

TIME UNTIL ARRIVAL:
15 MINUTES!

For a few moments, Hamish felt like he was part of an army.

His small gang of misfits and oddballs, in a weird dented Astral Plane, was flanked by **Belasko** choppers, armed with water cannons.

Belasko always had a plan when it came to Terribles, and today they would use their knowledge of the giant awfuls like never before. As you doubtless know by now, Terribles hate water – which made island living almost unbearable, to be honest. That was why they always took such great delight in taking to the mainland and running riot whenever possible.

The idea was that **Belasko** would use the choppers to soak those tankers in water, or create some kind of wall of water they couldn't get past, then the Terribles would panic. They'd want to get away as fast as possible. It had been

Lydia who had given them the idea: 'divide and conquer' she called it. Split up a pack and they lose the power of their numbers. Apparently, she'd done it tons of times with packs of marauding Tatzelwurms and Wolpertingers.

But Hamish was nervous about the **PDF** and Monster Patrol managing their part of the plan. He knew that maths was on their side, though. Elliot had even worked it out on a piece of paper.

> ONE MONSTER TO DEAL WITH = LESS THAN LOADS OF MONSTERS TO DEAL WITH

But this was a big monster. And if his and Luciana's dreams were right, then whatever it was, and whatever it looked like, it had some kind of connection with Hamish. He was the only one who could stop it.

The question was, how?

As they neared the cliffs, the choppers peeled off and flew towards **Frykt**, the thuds of their rotor blades heavy in the sky. Smasha slowed the Astral Plane and watched them fly away. Nobody said anything, but it was like their protection was getting smaller and smaller.

Thankfully, Hamish's dad broke the silence.

'We're not on our own,' he said, chewing his lip, a little nervously. 'We've got each other.'

Smasha began to guide the Astral Plane down towards the cliffs. The winter sky was clear this afternoon. Bright. Blue. Crisp. But in the distance, on the very edge of the horizon, grey clouds were beginning to swirl. Waters were becoming choppier.

'What's our plan, Grandma Lydia?' said Alice, leaping from the plane once it had landed. Everyone else followed hot on her heels.

'We'll know when it happens,' said Lydia. 'You know, the Monster Patrol motto is "Always Be Prepared".'

'Kit told us. And that's what *I* say,' said Alice, proudly.

'But look where that motto got me,' said Lydia. 'Captured by a flying peanut in a cave. You know, I'm starting to wonder if maybe life is about dealing with whatever's right in front of you. Believing you can do it. Maybe a better motto would be "Always Believe".'

Hamish and his dad stood at the edge of the cliffs.

'You've always come up with a plan in the past, pal,' he said. 'Maybe there's a way.'

'If he's the Chosen One, he'll find a way!' said Lydia, putting a hand on Hamish's shoulder.

Hamish's tummy turned and flipped. He couldn't help but wonder what would happen if he wasn't the Chosen One. I mean, wouldn't he feel more . . . *chosen*, by now if he was? Braver? In control? Wouldn't he be glowing or something? Also, who was doing the choosing? Chosen One Choosers needed to be a lot more forthcoming in their choices, Hamish thought, and maybe even provide a list of relevant reasons, just so everyone's on the same page.

Suddenly, from behind them, there came the most awful noise.

A sort of HUFFING, GRUNTING, STRAINING, GURNING, PUFFING, YUKKING noise.

Expecting the worst, Hamish turned round, only to let out a sigh of relief when he saw Grenville Bile on his mum's old tricycle. He was red-faced and out of breath and only halfway up the hill towards them. As usual, he was dressed in his elaborate El Gamba costume, which Clover seemed to have added about a million sequins to. El Gamba's logo was now in sparkly silver on his heaving chest and belly. He was cycling (or should that be tri-cling?) against the wind, which made his cheeks flap and his cape straight and his nostrils wide.

He must be here for a very important reason, thought Hamish.

'I was told there'd be cake!' yelled Grenville, when he finally reached them.

'What?' said Hamish.

'The **Belasko** catering tent is supposed to have cake,' Grenville said. 'They had a sign up and everything. They got a delivery. And it was free! But everyone from **Belasko** seems to have jumped in various vehicles and there's no one doing any catering whatsoever. I had to nick an old Twix out of a bin. But then someone told me you have sandwiches?'

'**LOOK!**' said Dad, suddenly, as halfway from the horizon, something was **TEARING** through the waves, seeming to slice the sea in two as it shot towards them.

'Bad time?' said Grenville.

And then Clover and Buster and Kit and Smasha and Venk all let out yelps as The Thing began to riiiiiiiise from the depths . . . thousands of small black fish falling from its head and body!

'I don't believe it,' said Lydia, staggering backwards, for the first time looking genuinely, heart-crunchingly, eye-sweatingly fearful. 'It's . . . no, it can't be . . . it's . . .'

30

IT'S HERE!!

'Well, I wasn't expecting THAT!' said Smasha. 'Seafood!'

'*You* can talk, fish face,' said Kit.

'Why is everyone constantly surprised I can talk?' said Smasha.

'This can't be!' said Lydia, open-mouthed and shaking her head.

'Well it can and it is,' said Grenville. 'You've got to be a realist.'

Hamish stared up at the mighty Prawn Kraken.

It was huge. And hideous.

How was he supposed to have a connection with *that*?

It was a hundred metres high. Armoured. With huge antennae that lashed out and CRACKED in the air like electrical whips.

The storm around it was intense, darkening the skies. Water lashed down around the **PDF** now, as Dad got on his walkie-talkie.

'Madame Cous Cous, activate the town clock!' he shouted. 'Engage missile mode. We're going to have to shoot this!'

But as lightning flashed around the gigantic monster, the electrical interference meant no one could be sure if the walkie-talkie was even working.

The Prawn Kraken let out a deafening . . .

ROOOOOOAR!

The air swelled with the thick, pungent stink of fish.

'Well . . . I'm going to leave you to it . . .' said Grenville, calmly, but his trike had toppled in the wind and flipped its way down the hill behind him.

As he turned, the Kraken spotted him and ROARED again. Have you ever walked past a fishmongers and been hit by that smell? Times that by a million!

'What do we do, Lydia?' asked Alice, holding her nose.

Lydia turned to Hamish.

'Remember in your dreams, you said you could see through the eyes of the monster. Try and remember, Hamish! What did you see?'

Hamish squeezed his eyes shut and tried to recall.

'Everyone's standing on the cliff,' he said.

'Good,' she said. 'And what happens?'

'I don't know,' said Hamish, struggling. 'That's all there is!'

'What do you *notice*?' said Lydia, with great urgency. 'When you took control of your dream, and you turned round, what did you see?'

The Prawn was getting ready to step on to the mainland. It could easily crush them underfoot. Under*feet*. And then it would go on a rampage through Starkley!

'I see a figure,' said Hamish, remembering, as his hair blew wild in the wind. 'Someone I didn't expect to be there. They're wearing something that's flapping around them. I thought maybe it could be Dad!'

He opened his eyes and looked to his dad, who was still trying to get through to someone on the walkie-talkie.

But as he did so, he noticed someone else.

Someone whose clothes were flapping in the wind, wildly and madly, just the way they had in his dream. It hit him in an instant.

'It's a *cape*!' he said, realising. 'I saw a cape!'

'Wait?' shouted Clover, over the noise of the wind. 'Are you saying . . .'

But no. It *couldn't* be. *Could* it?

'It's GRENVILLE!' yelled Hamish, pointing.

'GRENVILLE BILE IS THE CHOSEN ONE!'

This was not a sentence anyone had ever said before!

The ground thudded as the first of the prawn's legs made contact. The beast heaved itself from the water, its body shell **CRACKING** and CLICKING sickeningly! Hundreds of gallons of water crashed to the ground.

'**Grenville!**' urged Lydia. '**Take charge!**'

'What?' said Grenville. 'What am I supposed to do?'

'Fight it!' said Alice.

'**FIGHT IT?!**' said Grenville. 'It's five hundred times its size! You might as well ask me to fight *Sweden*!'

The monster had really spotted Grenville now. What was that tiny round baby prawn with its dangly antennae doing up here, on a cliff?

'Guys, thanks for the offer and all that, but I don't really want to be the Chosen One,' said Grenville, waving his arms in a 'No way!' motion – which just made all the little arms that Clover had sewn into his bodysuit do the same. 'No – Hamish is the Chosen One!'

'He's *Scarmarsh's* chosen one,' said Lydia. 'But the kid in the dream? The kid who saves Starkley? Scarmarsh doesn't get to choose *that* one!'

WH-CRACK!

The Kraken whipped its antennae above the group. As it snapped back, there was a flash of electrical impulse in the air. Its huge eyes were taking them all in. Stray, caught fish were falling from the cracks in its body and flapping to the ground.

'Oh no!' said Smasha, quickly picking them up and hurling them back into the sea as the Kraken watched, confused. 'Be free, my brothers!'

'Kit!' said Alice, urgently. 'You could use a spell!'

'What?' said Kit.

'Is a werewolf spell all you've got?'

'A *werewolf* spell?' said Hamish.

'Kit's a werewolf,' said Alice, like it was nothing. 'He asked me not to mention it. Sorry, Kit.'

'I'm *not* a werewolf,' said Kit. 'I could only *turn into* a werewolf because I had a werewolf claw. It's shapeshifting! But I don't have the claw with me!'

'Wait,' said Hamish, and there was that feeling he sometimes got . . .

The tingle . . .

The beginnings of an idea . . .

'So because you had the claw,' said Hamish, just to make certain, 'you could turn into a werewolf?'

'A *giant* werewolf!' said Alice.

'Well, yes,' said Kit. 'But guys – I don't have the claw!'

'Maybe you don't need the claw!' said Hamish. 'Does the spell work with other things?'

'I don't know!' said Kit. 'Maybe!'

Hamish looked around. Dad was bashing his walkie-talkie, willing it to work. Buster had his screwdriver out, trying to help him. Lydia was staring up at the Kraken, in total awe. Hamish had to try something.

Anything!

'What else have we got that we can use?' he said. 'Because Grenville is the Chosen One. He's the one who can take down that thing! What do we have for him?'

'How do you mean?' said Venk, confused.

'Has anyone got a spider on them? Can we catch a fly?' Hamish knew he was clutching at straws, but things were desperate!

'You want to turn me into a FLY?' yelled Grenville.

'I've got some sandwiches?' suggested Venk.

'Stop going on about sandwiches, Venk!' yelled Alice. 'I

know you probably feel like you haven't been doing much to help, but we cannot turn Grenville into a big sandwich! How could a big sandwich beat a massive prawn?'

'Funny you mention prawn, I've got prawn. Or cheese and onion?' said Venk, oblivious, taking them out of his jacket.

'Don't say they're prawn in front of a giant prawn!' cried Alice.

'Wait!' said Hamish, startled. 'Prawn?'

'It's only one prawn, because of rations,' said Venk, a little sadly. 'It's only a little one.'

'YES, Venk, you GENIUS!' yelled Hamish, grabbing the sandwich and ripping the cling film off. 'Kit, can you use the prawn the way you'd use a claw?'

'I . . . I don't know!' said Kit.

ROOOOOOAR!

The Kraken stepped forward.

'Of course you can,' said Hamish, encouragingly. 'Because you're Kit Alexander Lopez from Monster Patrol, and **you've GOT THIS!'**

The Kraken was towering over them, finding its bearings. It knew what it had to do. It had been *made* for this. Engineered for it. It could see Starkley so easily from here.

It STOMPED forward, crushing a bench. Its huge knees clashed against a lamp post which clattered to the ground and rolled past the gang, and off the edge of the cliffs.

'Watch out!' shouted Dad.

'It's now or never!' yelled Lydia.

'Grenville! HOLD THE PRAWN!' said Hamish.

'No thank you!' said Grenville, holding both hands up. 'I've been paying attention and this does not seem my scene at all!'

But Hamish grabbed Grenville's hand, stuck the prawn in it, and clenched the boy's fist tight around it.

'You can do this,' said Hamish, staring straight into Grenville's eyes. 'Don't you see? We're all here for a reason. You've been preparing all your life. Your obsession with El Gamba. Your wrestling. Your love of prawns. It was all for this *moment*!'

Grenville stared at him.

'You want me to wrestle a prawn?' he said, flatly.

'It's like you always say,' said Hamish. 'To be like the prawn, you have to think like a prawn! Now you get to do *both*!'

'We need to believe,' shouted Kit. 'We need to hold Grenville, and combine our belief! The more we believe, the stronger the spell!'

Everyone placed a hand on Grenville's sopping-wet costume.

'For the record, I did not agree to this!' he shouted.

THUD! The ground shook as the awful Kraken took another great step forward.

THUD! And another!

Kit started to nervously murmur his incantation, summing up whatever magic he could as the wind and the rain battered and pelted them. These were not ideal conditions!

And then . . .

A first small firework popped around them.

Shimmering and golden and gone in a heartbeat.

Kit strained as he tried to keep going.

'It's not working!' yelled Dad.

'Of course it's not working!' shouted Grenville. 'I'm just a boy holding a prawn on a cliff!'

'BELIEVE!' shouted Smasha.

'Yes!' yelled Alice. 'The more we believe, the more magic Kit can put into him! It's *science*! You can do it, my friend!'

But it wasn't just the gang who needed to believe it would work. It was Kit himself who needed to believe he could do it. It was *all* of them, together.

Hamish grabbed him by the shoulders.

'Remember!' he shouted. 'You are Kit Alexander Lopez of Monster Patrol! You protect the world! You have done this before! You can DO IT AGAIN!'

The **PDF** gritted their teeth and shut their eyes. They had to believe. In Kit. In each other. In the **PDF**. In Monster Patrol. For the sake of Starkley. They were a family, and this *had* to work.

Kit shuddered and said, 'GAH!' as more fireworks began to pop and fizz around him.

And then *more*.

Blues. Reds. Silvers. Golds. Purples.

Getting bigger, faster, stronger. Lasting longer, and longer.

'AND IT SHALL BE SO NOW!' shouted Kit, desperately.

'It's working, Kit!' said Hamish. 'I can feel it!'

And when he opened one eye to check, he was totally, utterly stunned to see what was happening to his old friend – to Grenville Bile, the Postmaster's son.

31

FIGHT! FIGHT! FIGHT!

It had started with a wobble.

The wobble had turned into a judder.

Then a wrench. And a twist. And a shaking of the wrist.

Grenville Bile had started to grow almost immediately.

His feet first.

Then his legs.

Then his tummy, stretching his poor El Gamba T-shirt to its very limits.

'What's happening to me?' he yelled, as Kit continued his murmuring, and ever-larger sparkling fireworks popped and burst on the air around him.

The **PDF** opened their eyes and stepped back, as right there in front of them, their classmate and friend continued to grow in the wind and rain.

'Keep going, Kit!' yelled Lydia. 'Continue the metamorphosis!'

'Meta morpha WHAT?' yelled Grenville.

Grenville was now bigger than Hamish's dad, and wasn't slowing.

'Metamorphosis,' explained Lydia. 'Therianthropy! Lycanthropy!'

'I'm not sure that's cleared it up!' shouted Grenville, whose voice was now booming.

'The Native Americans call it Skin-Walking,' said Lydia, who looked like she had never seen anything more wonderful in her life.

Above them, the Kraken stared curiously.

'Uh-oh!' boomed Grenville, who was now bright pink. **'Something else is happening!'**

In one quick FLASH, Grenville Bile no longer looked like Grenville Bile!

He had a sharp beak!

Big black eyes!

A hard shell!

He was . . .

Well, he was a PRAWN!

The Kraken unleashed a thundersome

ROAR.

What was this thing beneath it? It CRACKED its antennae, causing everyone on the cliff to dive for cover. Kit opened his eyes, and fell to the ground, exhausted.

'Did it work?' he said, blinking and trying to come to his senses.

'You turned Grenville into a big prawn!' shouted Elliot. 'So I'd say it worked!'

And Grenville had far from finished his shapeshifting.

His prawn legs had grown, giving him the balance he needed. His prawn arms had popped out, with giant claws on the end of each one. He grew . . .

And grew . . .

And gruesomely GREW!

And still around his vast neck – his tiny elasticated El Gamba cape!

'IT'S GRENZILLA!' shrieked Clover.

The Kraken had had enough. Whatever this creature was, it had to be dealt with! The Kraken worked on instinct. And instinct told it this thing was a threat.

It bellowed in rage, and began its attack, swiping at Grenzilla with its snapping claws.

But while the Kraken might have had its journey from the Gulf of Mexico to prepare for Starkley, Grenville had been preparing for this all his life.

All those wrestling videos on the internet. All that time spent reading about El Gamba. All those playground boasts and play-fights and time spent practising his moves on his bed. People had thought it was a stupid hobby, or that it was a waste of time. Well, no it wasn't. It was *training*!

Stingers!

PILEDRIVERS!

DOUBLE AXE HANDLES!

CHOP DROPS!

Throat thrusts!

Grenzilla was READY. He ducked, slowly but skilfully, and avoided the Kraken's clumsy punch.

Then Grenzilla launched himself at the Kraken and **POW**!

'**A European uppercut**!' said Alice, deeply impressed. She'd read all about this stuff in *Kickin' Butt* magazine.

POW AGAIN!

'Followed by a **spin kick**!' she said. She looked for all the world like one of those referees you see at wrestling matches, standing between the competitors, analysing it all.

'A monster battle,' said Lydia, now right by Alice's side, enjoying it just as much as her granddaughter was. 'You don't see many of these nowadays! They were all the rage once!'

The Kraken was stunned, but now ANGERED.

It whip-cracked its antennae at Grenville. It was like lightning striking a building. Smoke billowed from Grenzilla's shoulder, singeing his cape.

Well, that was NOT ON. Clover had spent ages on that cape. It was his pride and joy.

Grenzilla pounded towards the Kraken again, as the gang found cover behind the small block of public toilets by the cliff edge.

The Kraken extended its arms, ready to strike at the monster it had been sure had looked far smaller a few minutes ago. It would let it get just close enough and then trap it, and use its enormous beak to put an end to this.

'Careful, Grenville!' yelled Hamish. But at the last second, Grenzilla spun around, and . . .

PRAWN PUNCH!

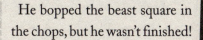

He bopped the beast square in the chops, but he wasn't finished!

'He's going for a **leg sweep**!' said Alice, as BOOM!

The Kraken fell to its side, its antennae lashing the ground and setting a tree on fire. Its legs spun around, trying to get a grip of the ground. But Grenzilla knew what it had to do. A classic wrestling finishing move!

In real life, Grenville had never done a prawn toss. I mean, who would really let Grenville practise his moves on them?

But he had studied it in intricate detail. He had obsessed over it. Watched it time and time again. Drawn pictures of it. School did not appeal to Grenville very much. He didn't like being told what he had to learn. But sometimes, the things you pick up outside of school – the things you really care about – can prove to be the most useful later on. And the El Gamba Prawn Toss was about to come in very useful indeed.

Would it be a Samoan Drop?

Would it be a Tombstone Piledriver?

Perhaps an Inverted Powerbomb?

No.

No, there was only one thing it could be.

'He's going to do an **EL GAMBA PRAWN TOSS**!' yelled Alice.

'A what?!' said Hamish's dad.

'It's his favourite Mexican wrestling move!'

Grenzilla pounced on the dazed and confused Kraken.

Folded his arms around it.

Squeezed it.

And using his very many legs for power, backflipped the Kraken, flinging it from the cliff edge and into the choppy waters below.

PRAWN TOSS SUCCESSFULLY EXECUTED!

The Kraken spluttered and ROARED as it tried to work out what it should do next. It stared up at Grenzilla, who was standing at the edge of the cliffs, looking all the taller and more powerful because of it.

Grenzilla ROARED now. And it was a roar that said one thing.

This is my town. Get lost!

The Kraken turned, and slunk away into the depths.

'You did it, Grenville!' shouted Hamish, in delight.

But Grenville did not understand him or reply, on account of him still being an enormous prawn.

'Grenville Bile – the Chosen One!' laughed Alice. 'Who would have thought it?'

Hamish's dad got straight back on the radio. He had to make sure the Terribles were being dealt with, and now that the electrical interference had disappeared with the Kraken, the walkie-talkies were back in action.

'Every kid is a Chosen One,' said Lydia. 'You just need to find out what you've been chosen for.'

And you would have thought everything would be all right now.

The monster that threatened Starkley was gone.

Belasko would have the Terribles surrounded and contained on their boats.

Lydia was back.

Venk still had spare sandwiches.

But Hamish stared out at the sea, not listening to the chatter of his pals.

Because the clouds were moving quickly, joining together

and blackening the sky.

This felt just like his dream. And that meant it wasn't over.

32

'HAAAAAAMISH,' came a voice.

It was a voice that dominated the sky.

It came from the sea, from the hills and fields and clouds.

It came from the left, the right, above them, below them.

It seemed almost to come from inside them.

The gang jumped and looked around.

'Is that . . . ?' asked Buster.

Hamish looked to the sky. To the place he'd flown in his dream, high above the cliffs. He felt that if Scarmarsh was watching him, he'd be watching him somehow from there.

How? He had no idea. A satellite? From a ship or plane? Or had Scarmarsh truly mastered magic? Was he some kind of God now? All-powerful?

'HAMISH!' it came again.

It was time for Hamish to face up to things and talk to Scarmarsh.

'What do you want from me?' he shouted into the wind.

'Why can't you just leave us all alone?'

Hamish's dad was watching, open-mouthed.

The voice of his brother. The brother he hadn't spoken to since that day so many years ago. The day Scarmarsh had found his name.

'YOU HAVE A GOOD HEART, HAMISH,' came the voice.

Hamish hadn't been expecting that . . . he didn't know what to say.

'Thank you?' he tried.

'BUT A HEART HAS TWO SIDES.'

'He's right,' whispered Elliot. 'It also has four chambers, the upper and lower.'

'I don't think that's what he means,' Clover whispered back.

'IT HAS A GOOD SIDE,' boomed Scarmarsh. 'THE SIDE WE ENJOY WHEN WE ARE YOUNG, AND FULL OF HOPE AND JUSTICE.'

Hamish looked at his friends in the **PDF**. At Lydia. His dad. Smasha and Kit. At Grenzilla. They really had to remember to turn him back into a boy.

'AND IT HAS A
BAD SIDE,' came the voice.
'AND THE BAD SIDE IS SO MUCH
MORE FUN.'

'Stop!' shouted Hamish's dad. 'Axel, he's not like
us! He shouldn't have to choose!'

What did his dad mean, 'us'? Was his dad saying he was
bad, too? That he'd had to decide to be good? Is that what
you do in life? You have to choose to be good?

'I KNOW YOU, HAMISH,' came the voice. 'AND
YOU ARE JUST LIKE ME.'

The fury swelled in Hamish's stomach.

'THE BAD SIDE WILL ALWAYS WIN,
HAMISH,' said Scarmarsh. 'THE BAD SIDE IS
WHERE TRUE POWER LIES. EVENTUALLY
YOU KNOW YOU WILL BE LEFT WITH
NOTHING. BUT JOIN ME, AND I CAN GIVE
YOU THE WORLD.'

How was Scarmarsh doing this? How did he seem to be
coming from everywhere? It didn't make sense. He *couldn't*
be all-powerful. But look at the evidence. He was nowhere,
yet he was everywhere. He was even in Hamish's dreams.
How could you fight someone like that? How could you

ever beat them? And could Scarmarsh be right – could even Hamish turn bad?

'YOU WILL JOIN ME, HAMISH,' said Scarmarsh. 'YOU WILL SIT AT MY SIDE. I WILL GIVE YOU THE WORLD.'

'That wasn't in my dream!' shouted Hamish. 'None of it!'

There was a pause.

No response.

That was weird.

He waited.

'AH, DREAMS,' came the reply, finally. 'PERHAPS ... YOUR DREAMS ARE TELLING YOU WHAT YOU ALREADY KNOW.'

Why had he taken so long to reply? And was Hamish imagining it, or did Scarmarsh sound a bit uncertain?

Hamish looked around. For the first time, he noticed a small CCTV camera on the public toilets at the edge of the cliff. The little red light underneath was blinking.

'PERHAPS YOUR DREAMS HAVE REVEALED TO YOU YOUR FUTURE.'

Scarmarsh seemed thrown by Hamish mentioning the dreams, almost as if he *didn't* know about them. And in that moment, Hamish knew the truth: his dreams were his *own*, they hadn't been created by anyone else. Somehow, he had known this day with Scarmarsh would come. Somehow, his *own mind* had been warning him.

And Hamish realised something else too: Scarmarsh was not all-powerful. He was a man, just like Hamish would be one day. Just like his dad was. And people made mistakes.

And if Scarmarsh wasn't some weird all-powerful God, then he had to be watching Hamish somehow. But what if it wasn't from the sky? What if it was through that camera? A normal man using tricks to make himself look impressive?

'Elliot,' whispered Hamish, covering his mouth so the camera couldn't see. 'What's the speed of sound?'

'Huh?' said Elliot. 'It's 343 metres per second.'

Hamish uncovered his mouth.

'SCARMARSH!' he shouted. **'Can I ask you something?'**

Hamish started to count in his head.

1 . . .

2 . . .

3 . . .

He kept counting. No response came.

And then . . .

'OF COURSE,' said Scarmarsh. 'ASK ME ANYTHING.'

This was the second time today Scarmarsh had actually said something in response. And it had taken him absolutely ages.

'Elliot,' whispered Hamish again. 'What's fourteen times 343?'

'Easy,' said Elliot. 'It's . . . a much bigger number. Why?'

'Cover your mouth! He can see us through that camera and read our lips!' said Hamish. 'Now, that reply took fourteen seconds. That means it *travelled* for fourteen seconds. If we can work out how many metres sound travels in fourteen seconds, then we can work out how far away he is!'

'What is this, H, maths class?' said Buster. 'What do you mean?'

'I think Scarmarsh is actually miles away,' whispered Hamish, his hand over his mouth, 'and he's using some kind of loudspeaker to project his voice to us. That's why it seems like it takes so long for him to reply – there's a delay!'

'It's 4802 metres!' said Smasha, quietly. 'Puffoxes are excellent with numbers.'

'*Brilliant!*' whispered Dad. 'That's about three miles.'

Hamish's eyes widened.

'That means he's either in Frinkley . . .' said Hamish.
'Or he's on **Frykt**.'

'Impossible,' said Dad. 'The **Belasko** agents have checked the island from the choppers. They saw Terribles, but no Scarmarsh.'

'Well, that's where the sound must be coming from,' said Hamish. 'Either he's on it, or his equipment is. That island is where his power lies. That's how he's doing this. And it's time we did something about it.'

Hamish's dad nodded. He knew just what Hamish was suggesting. One word had given it away. He stepped back, and took out his walkie-talkie, ready to give the order.

'WELL?' came Scarmarsh's voice again, still waiting for Hamish's big question.

And this time, Hamish did not scream into the sky.

He turned, and stared straight at the CCTV camera.

'Have you got the time on you, Uncle Axel?' he said, smiling.

33

The town clock shot through the air.

It had blasted off from the town square the very second Hamish's dad had given the order.

It had always been designed for a purpose just like this. But never did anyone think the target would be so close.

Belasko had immediately allowed the Terribles to flee on their boats and tankers. The choppers quietly escorted them away, pointing them towards the middle of the Atlantic Ocean. There were too many tankers to deal with, but rest assured: they *would* deal with them later.

For now, **Frykt** was the target, and Hamish and his pals watched as the town clock missile (Codename: the Time Bomb) arced through the air, tearing through clouds, and heading towards **Frykt**.

'I KNOW WHAT YOU'RE DOING!' screamed Scarmarsh, his voice reverberating around the cliffs.

If Hamish was right, he wouldn't be hearing Scarmarsh's voice for a while.

But was Scarmarsh on the island?

Or wasn't he?

Suddenly – a blinding light. Smasha covered his eyes. Buster yelped.

Hamish began to count.

1 . . .

2 . . .

3 . . .

And after fourteen seconds . . .

BOOOOOOOOOOOM.

Frykt was destroyed!

For a moment, everyone stood in silence.

Hamish glanced at the CCTV camera. There was no blinking red light any more.

'Scarmarsh?' called out Hamish. **'Uncle Axel?'**

He waited. Counted. Twenty seconds passed.

There was no response.

'It doesn't mean we got him,' said Dad. 'Just that we destroyed some of his equipment. He has other places. Other bases. He may just have been broadcasting the sound from **Frykt**.'

Hamish heard something in his dad's voice that sounded

almost hopeful. Like in some way he hoped Scarmarsh was okay. Hamish understood. Scarmarsh may have been the enemy, but he was also family. And his dad was right, Scarmarsh could have been anywhere even if the loudspeaker was on Frykt. But Hamish couldn't be certain. After all, would Scarmarsh really have given up the chance to see the Prawn Kraken take on Starkley? Could he have found a way of controlling it from the island? And would he have trusted the Terribles to assemble on their own?

Hamish had a feeling Scarmarsh wanted to destroy Starkley so that he would not only strike at the heart of **Belasko**, but leave Hamish with nothing. Perhaps if Hamish had nothing left to fight for, he would join him. But Hamish would never join Scarmarsh.

'We did something important today,' said Hamish. 'We showed Scarmarsh he can make mistakes. That he's not impossible to beat. And that we know it.'

'What if he does come back?' said Alice. 'What if we didn't get him? He always comes back harder.'

'Then we'll deal with him,' said Hamish. 'Together. As a team. Because we're the **PDF**.'

They high-fived.

And then very slowly everyone realised that Grenville Bile was still a massive prawn, and basically incapable of high-fives.

'I should probably do something about that,' said Kit.

When Smasha landed the Astral Plane back in the town square, things looked . . . well . . . a little different than they had.

'Goodness!' said Lydia.

The entire square was covered in soot from the town clock's rocket boosters. And the clock itself, of course, was missing.

'Maybe it's time we updated to digital anyway,' said Madame Cous Cous. 'Oh look – a delivery!'

A giant truck was rumbling into town, followed by supermarket vans and trucks.

The very second the Prawn Kraken had been dealt with, the barriers and gates had been raised all around Starkley. The townsfolk had pulled down the barbed wire in defiance. RULES SHEETS had been torn from buildings. Curfews had been banned. Extra-large shopping orders placed. They knew that, soon, the rest of the country would welcome it back with open arms – and indeed pretend like nothing had ever happened. The Central Speaker was playing easy listening music, and as if on cue, even the sun felt it was okay to shine again.

'CHIPS!' yelled Grenville, spotting someone happily walking past with a packet from Lord of the Fries. **'WE'VE GOT CHIPS AGAIN!'**

Grenville had no memory of being Grenzilla. It turned out that shapeshifting could be pretty traumatic the first time you try it and Grenville's brain had obviously decided the best way to cope was to block the whole wrestling match from his memory. He in no way believed that just an hour or so before, he'd been about the size of three double-decker buses, and bright pink. He just wondered where all his clothes had gone. Buster had lent him his pants, and at least he still had a cape. But he didn't care. Because Lord of the Fries was back, back, back!

'I'm getting scampi!' he shouted. 'For some reason I really feel like seafood. Sort of got the taste for it. Also I seem to stink of fish, which is weird. But I don't have any money on me!'

'I don't think you'll ever have to pay for a meal in this town again,' said Hamish's dad.

Grenville just looked at him like he was mad, and walked off.

The truck puffed and wheezed to a stop outside Madame Cous Cous's International World of Treats. It seemed ages since the kids had had a proper sweet shop blowout.

'You can take whatever you like,' said Madame Cous Cous, as the first barrel of Swedish Sweetballs was unloaded. 'But maybe avoid the candied prawns.'

'Grandma Lydia,' said Alice. 'Will you stay in Starkley? Please?'

Lydia smiled.

'I can stay a few days.'

'Just a few *days*?'

Lydia stroked her granddaughter's cheek.

'There's nothing I'd love more than to be right here with you and your mum,' she said. 'But so much time has passed since I last tried to settle down. And I'm needed elsewhere, now more than ever. If Scarmarsh is out there still, he'll be developing something even worse than he's managed so far. And these two need me.'

She pointed at Kit and Smasha, who were leaning against the Astral Plane.

'You can all stay!' said Alice. 'We could use you guys in the **PDF**! You can live in our HQ! People will get used to a big talking puffer fish walking around the place!'

'We have a job to do,' said Lydia. 'We're Monster Patrol. I need to teach Kit everything I know.'

'Teach *me!*'

'You have your own mission in life, Alice,' she said. 'You have to find out what it is. But make no mistake: you're a Chosen One too. I think you can choose to be a Chosen One. Every kid can. And I'd choose you every time.'

Alice smiled.

'I'm going to start up Monster Patrols everywhere I can,' said Lydia. 'The world needs it. And now we've got a Prawn Kraken to hunt!'

Alice knew there was no stopping this woman. She had a mission. It was just who she was. She'd never be a normal grandma.

'I'm going to do Monster Patrol properly this time. And I'm making Kit the Head of Magic.'

Kit looked delighted. Magic would live on, in Monster Patrol. He would learn everything he could. Not just about magic. But about his grandma. He had so many questions for Lydia. He could see that adventure ran in the family for both Hamish and Alice. He wondered what ran through his, and he wanted to find out.

'Our paths will cross again, my girl,' said Lydia. 'I

guarantee it.'

Alice hugged her grandma, hard, as the rest of the town poured into the square to congratulate their heroes. Hamish's mum. Jimmy. Alice's mum and dad, holding Benny the rabbit. Mr Slackjaw. A tiny squirrel called Flippy.

'Now, I've been eating coconuts for about twenty-seven blooming years,' said Lydia, 'is there *any* chance Venk could make me a sandwich?'

※

Well, they could do better than a sandwich.

The people of Frinkley, Thrupton, Urp and even Swellbelly immediately ordered all of their takeaway drivers and food trucks to get to their brave protectors in Starkley. They parked in the square in the shape of a big THANKS.

'Oh my WORD!' said Grenville Bile, running from truck to truck, with a vast teetering plate of burritos and curries and haddock and pizza and spring rolls and cheeseburgers and kebabs and chips and ice cream and . . .

'**PRAWNS!**' he shouted, dashing for a van called The Prawnbrokers.

He grabbed the biggest one he could and had a bite.

He went totally green.

'For some reason, I've gone off prawns,' he said, confused.

'I think I'm going to go vegan.'

Hamish took his food and sat down on the grass with his dad. The grass seemed greener now. It was like the whole town had had an injection of colour. What had been faded and grey was now vibrant again.

'That was fun,' said Hamish. 'I mean, it was absolutely horrific, but it was fun.'

'Which bit?' asked Dad. 'The Amazon? You have to tell me all about it!'

'Yeah, the Amazon was fun, except for the constant dangerous threats,' said Hamish. 'But I meant the last bit.'

'The Prawn Kraken? Or firing off the town clock?'

'No,' said Hamish. 'I mean, being on a mission with you.'

Hamish's dad smiled.

'Are some people just bad, Dad?' he said. 'What did you mean, on the cliffs, when you said "he's not like us"?'

'We all make choices,' he said. 'There's no such thing as an evil baby. Well, not any more, I mean. But sometimes weak people do bad things. The trick is to be brave enough to do the *right* thing. You still have many of those choices ahead of you. But something tells me you'll do the right thing.'

Hamish knew he was brave. He got scared sometimes, but he could be brave when it mattered. He looked over at

Lydia, making her daughter and granddaughter laugh at her incredible tales. He spotted Kit and Smasha, giggling with Grenville as they tried to convince him he'd spent much of the day being Grenzilla. He looked at Elliot and Clover and Buster and Venk and he felt an incredible warmth. Whatever happened, they were all going to be okay. Because they had each other.

'I want you to have something,' said Dad.

He reached into his pocket and pulled out a shiny silver **Belasko** badge.

'We don't really do medals,' he said. 'But I hope you'll think this is just as cool. I got it when I joined up.'

He pinned it on Hamish's jumper.

And Hamish liked it very much.

꙰

That night, exhausted, Hamish Ellerby fell onto his bed.

He wondered whether Scarmarsh would come to him in his dreams again.

He wondered whether he'd ever come back at all.

But he knew now that his dreams were his own, and he had dreamt of what he was scared of. He had been worried he was like his uncle.

Now he was more sure than ever that he was like his dad.

Hamish fell into a deep sleep, and can you guess what he dreamt of?

He dreamt of absolutely nothing.

THE END

for now . . .

LEARN SEAFOOD WRESTLING WITH...

GRENZILLA!

How to prang a prawn!

How to shrink a shrimp!

How to bustacean a crustacean!

**Wrestling seafood can be a tricky business.
Why not learn from the Chosen One?**

Includes one prawn ring and a fish paste medley.

SANDWICHES BY VENK!

Now that Starkley has access to the finest foods once again, why not try my new recipes?

NUT AND OLIVE!
PICKLE AND POPCORN!
CASHEW NIGHTMARE!
APPLE IN A BAP!
THE CHEESE BEAST!
MUM'S CURRIED MARS BAR!
THE MEATBALL MANIAC!

Available exclusively at the Queen's Leg, and everywhere else.

WANTED: A FAMILIAR

I am **NIT VILE** a nit enthusiast from Somerset and I need a Familiar so I can be in **MONSTER PATROL!** All I currently have is some nits that I have freed from various heads as part of my work in the **NIT LIBERATION FRONT!** Are you a **GIANT NIT?** Lots of people call **ME** a nit and I'm not sure why. Anyway, please be my Familiar and we can free nits together!!!

p11. Free Chips!
Starkley's got LOADS!

p23 - Unicorns real?!
Bold new claim!!

p24 - Po

NOW APPROVED BY THE PUBLIC OFFICE OF PRIDE (PO

Starkley Po

Wednesday 28st issue 13

MR SLACKJAW TO BE TEMPORARY TOWN CLOCK

Now that the town clock has been 'removed' (wink wink), there has been great debate as to what should replace it. Should we go digital? Should we use a sundial? Why don't we just Sellotape a watch to a lamp post?

Well, worry not! Garage owner Mr Slackjaw has agreed to stand where the clock used to be for fifteen hours a day, shouting out what time it is at random intervals.

Sadly, Mr Slackjaw did not turn up for his first day of work yesterday, because he lost track of the time.

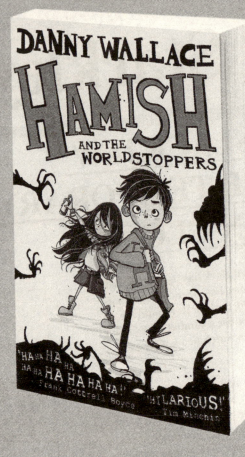

The people of Earth
are in BIG trouble again! Luckily
Hamish and his friends are here to
save the day ... aren't they??!

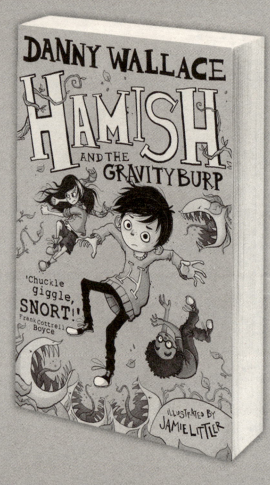

The whole town of Starkley is floating
on air… literally! Gravity has gone MAD
and Hamish is sure that the Terribles
and their evil master, Scarmash,
are behind the strange happenings …

DANNY WALLACE

HAMISH
AND THE
BABY
BOOM!

THE
BABIES
ARE COMING...
AND THEY'RE
RATTLED!

ILLUSTRATED BY JAMIE LITTLER

Beware the Babies ...

they CRY ...

they POO ...

they ATTACK!

Tis the season to be jolly,
but will this turn out to be a
TERRIBLE Christmas for Starkley?